"Liz, I think we need a do over."

Gabriel spied a bale of hay on the other side of the alley and pointed to it. "I'm going to sit down over there. When you're through with what you're doing, come sit with me and let's see if I can't make amends for upsetting you."

Her mouth opened, but she didn't speak. It was as if she was debating whether or not she wanted to listen to anything he had to say. Then she nodded. "All right. I'll put Cricket back in his stall, and then I'll be back."

He smiled. "I'll wait for you."

A minute later, Liz walked back and stopped in front of him. "Okay, here I am. What do you want to talk to me about?"

"I want..." he began, but the words froze in his mouth at the sight of a red laser dot focused on the center of Liz's forehead.

With a strangled cry, he lunged from the hay bale, tackled her around the legs and fell to the ground on top of her just as a bullet whizzed past their heads.

Sandra Robbins is an award-winning, multipublished author of Christian fiction who lives with her husband in Tennessee. Without the support of her wonderful husband, four children and five grandchildren, it would be impossible for her to write. It is her prayer that God will use her words to plant seeds of hope in the lives of her readers so they may come to know the peace she draws from her life.

Books by Sandra Robbins

Love Inspired Suspense

Smoky Mountain Secrets

In a Killer's Sights
Stalking Season
Ranch Hideout

Bounty Hunters

Fugitive Trackdown
Fugitive at Large
Yuletide Fugitive Threat

The Cold Case Files

Dangerous Waters
Yuletide Jeopardy
Trail of Secrets

Visit the Author Profile page at Harlequin.com for more titles.

RANCH HIDEOUT

SANDRA ROBBINS

H HARLEQUIN® LOVE INSPIRED® SUSPENSE

Recycling programs
for this product may
not exist in your area.

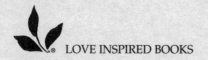 LOVE INSPIRED BOOKS

ISBN-13: 978-0-373-45701-4

Ranch Hideout

Copyright © 2017 by Sandra Robbins

All rights reserved. Except for use in any review, the reproduction
or utilization of this work in whole or in part in any form by any
electronic, mechanical or other means, now known or hereinafter
invented, including xerography, photocopying and recording, or in
any information storage or retrieval system, is forbidden without
the written permission of the editorial office, Love Inspired Books,
195 Broadway, New York, NY 10007 U.S.A.

This is a work of fiction. Names, characters, places and incidents are
either the product of the author's imagination or are used fictitiously, and
any resemblance to actual persons, living or dead, business establishments,
events or locales is entirely coincidental.

This edition published by arrangement with Love Inspired Books.

® and TM are trademarks of Love Inspired Books, used under license.
Trademarks indicated with ® are registered in the United States Patent
and Trademark Office, the Canadian Intellectual Property Office and in
other countries.

www.Harlequin.com

Printed in U.S.A.

The Lord is my strength and my shield; my heart trusted in Him, and I am helped: therefore my heart greatly rejoiceth; and with my song will I praise Him.
–Psalms 28:7

To my husband who's always there to support and help me

ONE

Liz Madison realized her mistakes too late. First, she shouldn't have dawdled in the theater lobby studying the posters for coming attractions when the movie was over. By the time she exited the building, the parking lot had emptied, and her car sat in its lone spot in the late afternoon's gathering darkness. Second, she really should have been more attentive to her surroundings. If she had been, she would have heard the man's footsteps behind her, and she could have made a run for it.

Now she found herself pressed face-first against the driver's side of her car with her hands splayed against the window, her keys dangling from her fingers. A choking sound escaped her throat as a hand tightened around her neck, and her attacker pressed a gun against her head.

A sudden gust of wind swished her long skirt around her legs, but she trembled more from fear than from the cold. A man's face rubbed against her cheek, and the fabric of the ski mask he wore scratched her skin. The smell of tobacco assaulted her senses as his warm breath rippled over her face. "Don't make a noise, lady, or it'll be the last one you ever make."

Liz closed her eyes and tried to keep from retching. "Wh-what do you want?"

"Let's start with your money," he said. His body kept her pinned against the car as one hand pushed the gun harder against her head and the other rifled through her jacket pockets. He pulled her cell phone out and threw it to the ground before he reached back in for her wallet.

The reprieve of his hold on her neck gave her the opportunity to glance over her shoulder. His attention was directed to the cash in her wallet. A moment later, he snorted in disgust, and the gun pressed against her head again.

"Fifty dollars?" he snarled. "You only carry fifty dollars?"

"I—I never carry much money," she answered.

He didn't say anything for a moment. Then he laughed. "Well, I was thinking we'd take a little drive anyway. I see you have a debit card. Maybe we'll make a stop first at your bank. You can go through the ATM and get some cash."

"No, please," she begged. "Just take the money and go."

The gun dug harder into her temple, and she closed her eyes in anticipation of the bullet that was about to end her life. He chuckled and brought his mouth back to her ear. "It's either go to the ATM, or we'll end it right here with a bullet."

"I-if I go to the ATM and give you the money, will you let me go then?"

He chuckled. "Sure I will."

The mocking tone of his voice told her he had no intention of letting her go. If she left the parking lot with him, he would kill her. The wilderness of the Smoky Mountains provided the perfect spot to dispose of a body that might never be found. And to think, she had come here to be safe—to escape from the danger she'd left back home. How ironic.

Liz pressed her hands against the car window harder to keep from collapsing. If she was to live, she had to do something. But what?

The man released her neck and grabbed hold of her arm. "Now, don't make a sound as we get in the car. If you do..."

Before he could follow through on his threat, his grip on her released, and he let out a strangled cry of pain. Out of the corner of her eye she saw him fall to the ground, and she whirled to see what had happened.

A man she'd never seen before bent over her attacker. She gasped as the mugger raised his gun. Before he could fire, her rescuer delivered a swift kick, and the weapon sailed across the pavement. He then slammed his foot down on her assailant's arm and pinned it to the ground as he reached down, grabbed the man's shirt tight enough to pull his head up and delivered a solid blow to his jaw. Her attacker fell back unconscious.

The stranger reached for the gun on the ground and tucked it into the waistband of his jeans before he turned to her. "Are you all right?"

She pressed her hand to her chest and nodded. "Yes, but if you'd been a few seconds later, I don't think I would have been."

"You're safe now." He directed his attention back to the man still on the ground, but he hadn't moved.

He picked up her cell phone. "Is this yours?"

She nodded, and he handed it to her before he pulled his from his pocket and punched in 911. "My name is Gabriel Decker. I'm at the Cinema Theater. A man attacked a woman in the parking lot, and I've subdued him. I need officers right away."

He paused as he listened to the voice on the phone before he spoke again. "Thanks."

He ended the call and looked down at his prisoner, who was just beginning to stir. "I've called the police," he told the mugger. "They'll be here in a few minutes. Until then, if I were you, I wouldn't try anything stupid. I know how to use a gun, and I'll pull the trigger if you move a muscle."

With one swift movement he reached down and jerked the mask from the man's face. Liz took a step back to distance herself from the cruel eyes that glared up at her. She'd heard the expression *if looks could kill* many times, but she'd never seen such hatred on anyone's face.

"Do you know this guy?" Gabriel's voice penetrated her thoughts, and she shook her head.

She might not know him, but the threat she'd heard in his voice had set off warning bells in her head. She knew he'd meant to kill her. Had he picked her at random to target in a parking lot, or was it something more? Had the trouble she'd left behind found her again?

She slowly shook her head. "No, I've never seen him." It had to be just a coincidence that she'd been attacked. She couldn't allow this random crime to make her paranoid or she'd never feel safe going anywhere again.

The sound of a siren split the air, and a squad car with its lights flashing rolled into the parking lot. Two men jumped out and walked toward them. She recognized them right away. She'd met Sheriff Ben Whitman and his deputy Luke Conrad soon after she'd come to Sevier County a few weeks ago.

Sheriff Whitman frowned as his gaze swept over her. "Are you okay, Liz?"

She nodded. "I am, thanks to Mr. Decker."

He turned his attention to her rescuer, who stuck out his hand. "Gabriel Decker, Sheriff. I'm the one who made the call to 911."

Sheriff Whitman shook his hand and then tugged the brim of his Stetson lower over his eyes. "And where were you when this was taking place?"

"I had just come out of the theater when I saw the man push her against her car. I rushed over as fast as I could."

"That was quick thinking."

Gabriel shrugged. "Well, I knew it wasn't a friendly encounter when I realized he had that gun pressed to her head. I'm just glad I could help."

Deputy Conrad reached down and yanked the man to his feet. "Face the car and put your hands behind your back."

Her attacker delivered another withering glance her way before he did as the officer ordered. When Luke had snapped handcuffs on him, he searched the man's pockets for some identification. After a moment, empty-handed, he looked at the sheriff and shook his head.

"What's your name?" Luke demanded.

His question was met with silence. "I'll ask you again. What's your name?" Still nothing.

Ben shrugged. "So he wants to play hardball. Well, we can, too. Read him his rights, Luke, and put him in the backseat of the squad car." He watched until Luke had their prisoner secured, then turned back to her. "I've heard Mr. Decker's account. Now tell me yours, Liz."

For the next few minutes she related what happened from when she left the theater until the officers arrived. She ended by glancing at Gabriel Decker. "I really believe he meant to kill me. If Mr. Decker hadn't come along, I—I d-don't know..."

She couldn't finish her sentence, and she covered her face as tears began to roll from her eyes. Ben Whitman stepped closer and patted her on the shoulder. "You're safe now. I'm going to do everything I can to see that he stays in jail for a long time."

Liz looked up at him through tear-filled eyes. "Do you think he might be..." She clamped her lips together and darted a glance at Gabriel Decker. He was a stranger, and she'd almost revealed too much.

Sheriff Whitman squeezed her shoulder and smiled. "Don't worry about that now. He's probably already in the system—we'll know more once we run his fingerprints. We'll find out who he is."

Liz wanted to believe him, but she couldn't. She had thought she was safe in this mountain community, but she hadn't been this afternoon. The fact that her assailant had no identification concerned her even more. This whole encounter reeked of a professional hit. Had they found her? Was she in danger?

She pulled her attention back to Sheriff Whitman when she realized he'd said something. "I'm sorry. What did you say?"

"I asked if you're okay to drive home, or do you want one of us to do it?"

Before she could answer, Gabriel Decker spoke up. "Sheriff, I'd be glad to follow her home and see that she gets there safely."

An uncertain look flashed across Ben's face, and he frowned. "I don't know…"

Before the sheriff could finish, Gabriel Decker smiled at her. "Do you live nearby?"

"It's a few miles out of town. I wouldn't want to detain you if you have other plans for the evening."

He shook his head. "No, I don't have anywhere to be. I'll just follow you and see that you get there safely."

Liz started to decline. Gabriel Decker may have saved her life this afternoon, but she knew nothing about him. However, there was something about the way his dark eyes stared at her that gave her the feeling she could trust him. Before she realized what she was saying, she spoke. "That's very kind of you. I appreciate it."

Sheriff Whitman glanced back at Luke in the idling squad car and nodded. "Then we'll get back to the station and get this guy booked. I'll talk to you in the morning, Liz."

"Okay, and thank you."

He smiled and waved his hand in dismissal. "No need to thank me. That's what we're here for."

She watched as he strode toward the car and got in. Then Luke drove them from the parking lot. With the absence of the revolving lights on top of the police car, the area darkened, and Liz shuddered. Next time she came to the movie, she was going to park in a more central location. That is, if she ever came again.

It was as if Gabriel Decker read her thoughts. "I'm sorry for what happened to you today, but you really should park in a more visible spot."

Liz nodded. "I think I've learned my lesson."

He cocked his head to one side and studied her. "The next time you should bring someone with you. A friend, or maybe your boyfriend."

She chuckled. "I would if I had any friends here, but I'm new to this area. I haven't had time to meet many people yet." Then she realized she hadn't introduced herself. She held out her hand. "I'm Liz Madison, by the way."

He wrapped his fingers around hers. "I'm Gabriel Decker." They stood that way for a moment before he cleared his throat and dropped her hand. "I must say our first meeting was different than any I've had before."

Liz laughed. "For me, too." She reached for the handle to open the car door. "I hope following me home isn't taking you out of your way. Do you live around here, Mr. Decker?"

He shook his head. "Call me Gabriel, please. And no, I don't live here. I'm staying at Little Pigeon Ranch for a few weeks, taking a breather before I begin a new job. I've always loved visiting the Smokies and thought it would be a good place to relax."

She stopped and stared at him in surprise. "You're staying at Dean and Gwen Harwell's ranch? So am I."

He grinned and looked down at her again, and she realized that her head barely came up to his shoulders. "It's good to meet another guest. How long have you been here?"

"Only a few weeks, but I love it. Actually, I'm more of a working guest. Dean is letting me help with the horses and do some riding lessons and trail rides. I'm really enjoying it. When did you arrive?"

"Just this afternoon. I came into town to see what it was like and decided to go to the movie when I saw what was playing."

Liz arched her eyebrows and glanced at him. "You wanted to see a chick flick?"

He shrugged. "What can I say? I'm a romantic at heart."

The teasing way he said it made her smile. "Somehow I find that hard to believe."

He glanced around as if checking to see if anyone could hear. "No, I'm serious." He lowered his voice to a whisper. "My favorite movie is *Pride and Prejudice*, but don't tell anyone. I wouldn't want it to tarnish my masculine image."

She rolled her eyes and smiled. "Now I know you're kidding."

"I promise I'm not," he said as he reached over and pulled her car door open. "You said you help with the horses at Little Pigeon. Do you like to ride as much as you like chick flicks?"

"Riding is my favorite thing," she said. "I've been riding since I was a little girl."

"I grew up on a ranch in Texas, so I've ridden all my life, too. Maybe we can ride together sometime while I'm at Little Pigeon."

Her face grew warm, and she bit down on her lip. "Maybe."

He grinned and winked at her. "Good. I do love to ride. It ranks right up there with *Pride and Prejudice*."

She burst out laughing, and he continued to grin as she climbed into her car. Within minutes she was on the road to the ranch with Gabriel following. As she drove, she thought about the man who had come to her rescue and said a prayer of thanks that he was there when she needed him.

She wondered what kind of work he did. He said he was taking a breather from his job but not what that job was. He really hadn't revealed too much about himself, but that wasn't surprising. She hadn't either, and she wasn't about to, even though he seemed like the kind of man who could be a good friend. His quick wit when he teased her about being a romantic and his volunteering to follow her home caused her mouth to quirk in a slight smile.

Suddenly she stiffened and tightened her fingers on the steering wheel, the smile now completely gone from her face. What was she thinking? She couldn't have a friend. One of the conditions of her being here was that nobody was to know who she was or why she'd come to Dean and Gwen's ranch. She had to guard her relationships very carefully. One slipup about her true identity could be disastrous for a lot of people. Especially for her.

She looked up in the rearview mirror and caught a glimpse of his car behind her. No matter how grateful she was for his help earlier, she knew what she had to do—stay away from him as long as he was at Little Pigeon Ranch.

Gabriel's gaze darted back and forth across the road as he followed Liz back to the ranch. His protective instincts were on high alert today, and his stomach clenched at the thought of what would have happened if he hadn't been at the movie. His heart had skipped a beat when he saw the gun pressed to her head. He'd known there was no way she could escape the hold of a man who had to outweigh her by at least a hundred pounds. The thought had flashed through his mind that she was much more petite than what she looked like in the pictures from her official file.

The first time he'd seen a photograph of her, he'd been struck by her eyes. Their blue color reminded him of the waters he'd once seen off the coast of Bermuda, crystal-clear blue with just a tint of green. They were even more striking when seen in person. Her hair, which was held in place with a clip on top of her head, looked almost like a golden crown that sparkled in the dusk light. All in all, he'd have to say she was one of the most beautiful women he had ever seen.

Her friendly manner wasn't at all what he'd expected, though. He'd expected to find a person who was private and suspicious. Most people in her position would react that way, but not Liz. Maybe the way they'd met, with him saving her, had been the key to allaying her suspicions. That was promising, since he needed her to trust him.

These thoughts were still running through his head when the ranch came into sight. She pulled up beside the house, and he pulled up behind her. Before he could step from the car, she was already hurrying toward the front of the house.

"Thanks again for your help. I really appreciate it," she called out to him.

"Wait!" he yelled as he jumped from the car. He caught up to her at the bottom of the porch steps. "Liz, I'd like to—"

Before he could finish his sentence, she interrupted him. "I hope you enjoy your stay at Little Pigeon. Dean has all kinds of activities planned for his guests. There's a schedule in the office, and you can sign up for whatever interests you."

"I'm not much into planned excursions. I like to explore on my own, but I'll take a look." He paused for a moment before he continued. "Maybe you'd like to show me around the area. We could go for a ride."

Her forehead wrinkled as she studied his face. "I don't know," she finally said. "I stay busy. Don't have much leisure time. This afternoon was the first time I've been able to get away all week."

He nodded. "I understand, but I'll check with you and see."

"Okay." She glanced at her watch. "I have to go now.

I told Gwen I'd help with dinner for the guests, and I'm running late."

"Then go on," he said. "I'm eating in the dining room tonight, so I'll see you then."

A shaky smile pulled at her mouth. "We'll see." She backed away a few steps. "It was nice meeting you, Gabriel. I'll see you later."

"Nice meeting you, too, Liz."

She didn't say anything else, and he watched as she climbed the steps to the porch. Her demeanor had changed dramatically on the way back from town. She'd seemed more closed off once they'd gotten back to the ranch. It was almost as if the girl with the smiling eyes he encountered in the movie parking lot had disappeared and been replaced with a skittish woman who wasn't quite sure about the stranger she'd met.

He narrowed his eyes and wondered if he had come on too strong for their first meeting. Maybe the best thing to do would be to give her some time for a day or two to get used to his presence here. Once she became accustomed to seeing him in the dining room and around the barn, she might feel more at ease with him. The last thing he needed was her running away every time she saw him. He couldn't keep her safe if she wouldn't let him near her.

When she reached the front door, she glanced over her shoulder and straight at him. He didn't know if he imagined it or not, but her step appeared to falter for a moment. No doubt about it. She was suddenly nervous around him. He was going to have to do something about that.

His supervisor was trusting him to ensure no harm came to Liz before she could testify against a criminal kingpin. He was also trusting Gabriel to handle the assignment discreetly. If Liz knew that the FBI had assigned her a protective detail, she'd want to know why… and the answer might make her change her mind about the wisdom of testifying. That would be a disaster. He had to get this just right—had to keep her safe, no matter what…and he had to do it without letting her ever suspect that he was an FBI agent.

"You may call yourself Liz Madison, but I know who you really are, Elizabeth Madison Kennedy," he muttered under his breath as she disappeared into the house. "So you'd better get used to me. I'm going to be around for a while."

TWO

Liz put the last of the dirty plates in the dishwasher and glanced around the kitchen to see if she'd missed anything. Tonight they'd had more guests for dinner than usual. She'd stayed in the kitchen, but several times she'd stood at the door into the dining room and listened to bits of the guests' conversations. The room had buzzed with chatter about trail rides, excursions to Cades Cove or hiking adventures on the Appalachian Trail.

This was just the beginning of the fall tourist season when the mountains came alive with brilliant colors. Once the leaves had faded, the holiday festival of lights would take over and draw thousands of tourists. Gwen said Little Pigeon Ranch was booked solidly to the end of the year. Liz couldn't wait to participate in all the festivities.

She paused in closing the dishwasher and shook her head. What was the matter with her? She wouldn't be here to see those things. If all went as she hoped, she'd be back in her apartment in Memphis soon, and her life would settle back into the routine she'd enjoyed before coming here.

The door between the dining room and the kitchen suddenly swung open, and Liz jerked her head around to see Gwen storming into the kitchen. She stopped just inside the room and placed her hands on hips. "Why didn't you tell me you were attacked in the theater parking lot?"

The muscles in Liz's throat constricted as she tried to swallow. "I'm sorry, Gwen. I didn't have a chance. When I got here, you were in the middle of getting dinner ready to serve, and we've been busy ever since."

Gwen pursed her lips and shook her head. "That's no excuse, Liz. You know that Dean and I need to be informed if anything happens to you."

"And I was going to tell you. I just haven't had time." Liz paused as a thought struck her, and she frowned. "How did you find out?"

Gwen's expression softened as she studied her. "Mr. Decker told me."

Liz's eyes widened in surprise. "He told you? When?"

"While he was eating dinner. I stopped at his table to see if he had everything he needed. He asked where you were, and I told you were in the kitchen." Gwen arched an eyebrow. "Is he the reason you didn't come out of the kitchen all during dinner?"

"No!" Liz blurted out without thinking. "I mean, I was busy."

Gwen stared at her for a moment before she took Liz by the hand and led her to the kitchen table. When they were both seated, she leaned forward and squeezed Liz's hand. "When something like this happens, you have to tell us about it."

"I don't think it was related to my testimony," Liz offered. "I honestly think he was just a creep trying to rob me. I was just in the wrong place at the wrong time—again."

"Maybe," Gwen said. "But maybe not. Dean and I can't help protect you if we don't know what's going on. We feel a responsibility to take care of you while you're here."

Liz shook her head. "I know you do, and I'm sorry about putting that burden on you. I worry all the time about how I've brought my problems to your and Dean's doorstep. If anything happened to you or Dean or to your daughter…" She stopped, unable to go on as tears filled her eyes.

Gwen's pressure on her hand increased. "Don't worry about us. We agreed to this fully aware of the risks. It's your safety we all have to focus on."

The tears pooling in Liz's eyes blurred her vision, and she tried to blink them back. "I feel like I'm taking advantage of you and Dean. You've offered me a safe haven for now, and I don't want you to regret it."

"We would never regret it. I can't even imagine what you've been through. We just want to help you."

Her chest tightened. "You have. More than you'll ever know." She took a deep breath and wiped at her eyes. "Now I need to finish up in here. I've cleaned the countertops and the stove. All I need to do is sweep the floor, and I'll be through."

Gwen shook her head. "I'll do that. You need some

time to get over what happened this afternoon. You enjoy your time painting at night. Go on up to your room, and I'll see you in the morning."

Liz sighed as she stood up, took off the apron she was wearing and hung it on a peg next to the refrigerator. "I don't think I'll paint tonight. I think I'll go on to bed. I want to get up early so I can help Dean muck out the stalls in the morning."

Gwen pushed up from her chair and propped her hands on her hips. "Liz, you're doing too much around here."

"I like helping out," Liz insisted. "It takes my mind off things."

"You can't keep busy forever," Gwen said gently. "You aren't going to be able to come to terms with what happened until you talk about it. I can find you a Christian counselor if you'd like."

Liz sniffled and looked down at the floor. "I do need to talk, to release these pent-up feelings that are driving me insane. But I don't want to tell some stranger." She raised her head to stare into Gwen's eyes. "Since I've been here, I've become closer to you than anybody else. Maybe I need to tell you about it."

"Whenever you're ready, Liz, I'll listen."

"Thanks, Gwen. I appreciate it."

They stared at each other for a moment before Gwen smiled and pulled Liz into a hug. "Now you go on to bed, and don't worry about anything tonight. We'll get through this one day at a time."

Liz let out a grateful sigh as she hugged Gwen. She was so blessed that the FBI had persuaded Dean and Gwen to take in a stranger who needed protection.

They'd accepted her without question, and she would never forget it.

After a moment she released Gwen and walked from the room. As she trudged through the dining room, she caught sight of Gabriel Decker sitting at a table alone. He sipped from a coffee cup and stared at her over the rim.

Before she could make her escape to the hallway, he called out to her. "Liz, I missed you during dinner. Mrs. Harwell said you were in the kitchen."

She stopped and turned to face him. She wanted to reproach him for telling Gwen about the parking lot incident, but she had trouble holding on to her annoyance with him at the sight of his beautiful smile, which reached all the way up to his eyes. "I was. We had a lot of guests tonight, and I helped the cook with the meal."

He pointed to the chair across from him. "Would you like to sit and have some coffee with me?"

She lifted her chin and stared down her nose at him. "No, thanks. I'm tired and going to bed."

"Will I see you tomorrow?" he called out as she stepped into the hall.

"Maybe." She stopped halfway up the stairs and glanced back over her shoulder.

He had risen and followed her into the hall. He stood at the foot of the stairs with his hand on the banister. "I'll look for you."

The words were innocent enough on the surface, but her breath still froze in her chest. Back in Memphis there were plenty of dangerous people looking for her, and Gabriel's remark had served as an unpleasant reminder of the danger she was still in. It was all she could do to make her legs climb the remaining stairs to the second floor. When she glanced back down, he was still standing there, his eyes on her.

She stiffened at the panic that spread through her body. Why was he being so friendly, and how was it that he just happened to be in the parking lot when she was attacked? Perhaps he wasn't just a guest who had come to spend a few weeks at Little Pigeon. Maybe he'd come there looking for her.

Biting down on her tongue to keep from crying out, she rushed to her room, ran inside and locked the door. Then she leaned against it and closed her eyes as she tried to control her breathing. What was happening to her? Was she right to be scared, or was she overreacting? It was hard for her to trust anyone. She saw ulterior motives in even the most innocent of other people's actions. She couldn't go on like this much longer.

A whimper escaped her throat as she slid down the door until she was sitting on the floor, her legs bent and her arms circling her knees. She had to do something, or she was never going to make it through the next few months.

Maybe Gwen was right. She needed to talk to someone, and Gwen had offered. Now all she had to do was make herself do it. She gritted her teeth. She couldn't put it off any longer. She would tell Gwen everything that happened that day, and she would do it tomorrow.

Gabriel watched Liz until she got to the top of the stairs before he turned around and walked back into the dining room. He sat down and picked up his coffee cup and stared at it for a moment.

"Something wrong with the coffee?" The voice behind him startled him, and he swiveled in his seat to see who it was. He relaxed when he saw that it was Dean Harwell.

He laughed and set the cup down. "The coffee's fine. In fact, everything I ate for dinner was delicious. If that was any indication of the caliber meals you serve here, I may want to move in."

Dean chuckled and slid into the seat across from him. "The cook here started working for my grandfather when I was growing up. We couldn't get along without him."

"I can see why," Gabriel said as he pushed his plate aside and crossed his arms on the table. "So what have you been up to tonight?"

"I was out at the barn taking care of a few chores. Seems like there's always something needing to be done."

Gabriel chuckled and nodded. "I remember how it was when I was growing up on a ranch. Sometimes I think about getting a little piece of land and a few horses. I guess that won't ever happen, though. In my job it's possible I could be transferred at any time, so I'm afraid to put down any roots that I might have to leave behind."

Dean studied him for a moment before he glanced over his shoulder and scanned the room. When he didn't see anyone, he leaned closer and lowered his voice. "I haven't had a chance to talk to you about your job since you arrived earlier, but we're alone now."

Gabriel nodded his agreement. "I was hoping I'd get a chance to see you tonight. Especially after what happened today."

Dean's eyes grew large. "What are you talking about?"

"The attack on Liz."

"Attack?" Dean's voice seemed to bounce off the wall, and Gabriel leaned in farther.

Gabriel raised his index finger to his lips to quiet Dean. "I thought your wife had told you about it."

"No. When did you tell Gwen?"

"Not too long before you came in. But you can relax. Everything turned out all right."

For the next few minutes Dean didn't move as Gabriel recounted what had happened in the theater parking lot. When he finished, Dean's eyebrows drew together as he stared across the table at Gabriel.

"I've been afraid something like this might happen. When I got a call from my old friend Bill Diamond in the Memphis FBI office wanting me to offer Liz a safe place to stay, I was uncertain what to do. I didn't want to endanger my family. Bill promised me that wouldn't happen, that you are one of his top agents."

"I don't know about being one of the top agents, but I'm dedicated to my job, Dean. I've been with the FBI for five years now, and I really like my work. I'll do everything in my power to make sure nothing bad happens to anybody at Little Pigeon while I'm here. I'm sorry I couldn't be here when Liz first came, but I was finishing up another case. Bill assured me that since you are a former police officer, you would be able to protect Liz until I could get here."

"There haven't been any threats until today. I'm glad you arrived before she left and could follow her to the movie. It might have turned out differently if you hadn't."

"Maybe so."

Dean sat back in his chair and cast a quizzical look at him. "Why was the decision made for you to go undercover while you're here? Maybe Liz would feel more at ease if she knew she had an FBI agent here to protect her."

Gabriel rubbed the back of his neck and sighed. "Daniel Shaw's trial has all of us on edge. She's the first witness who has agreed to testify who can directly connect him to a crime. If we can put him away, we have a better chance of taking down the rest of his gang. We've got to make sure Liz testifies. One of our snitches passed us some information that Shaw's gang isn't happy about his arrest and they're going to try to keep Liz from testifying." Gabriel paused, wondering if he should share the next part, then pressed on. "There's a price on her head—a fairly high one. There's some concern in the office that she might decide to take off if she found out. She has no family, no ties. If she decides to run, our whole case goes out the window. Bill decided we had to have agents here protecting her."

Dean nodded. "Bill didn't tell me the name of the other agent. What is it?"

"Her name is Andrea Cauthorn. She's arriving tomorrow. Bill didn't want there to be anything to tie us together, so he wanted her to arrive a day after I did. She'll help me keep an eye on Liz. Then when the trial date arrives, we'll escort her back to Memphis."

A look of concern flashed in Dean's eyes, and he tilted his head to one side. "Do you think the guy who attacked her today could have ties to Shaw's gang? Or maybe have heard about the price on her head?"

"I don't know. He had no identification on him, but Ben's going to check it out. He'll let us know if he finds out anything."

Dean frowned. "I don't like this. If that guy was specifically after Liz, that means they know where she is."

"I don't see how they could have that information. The only ones at our office who know Liz's whereabouts are Bill, Andrea and myself. We'll be on our guard all the time." He paused for a moment. "Don't worry, Dean. We don't intend for any harm to come to your family or anybody else at Little Pigeon."

Dean nodded. "Thanks, Gabriel, but you know I'll also be on guard to make sure that doesn't happen."

A smile pulled at Gabriel's mouth. "I guess once a cop, always a cop."

"Yeah," Dean said. "I was a cop, and a good one. But that's not as important to me now as being a husband and a father. I don't want anything to happen to my family, or to my employees and guests either."

"Neither do we."

Gwen walked out of the kitchen at that moment. When she saw Dean sitting at the table, she smiled and crossed the room to where they sat. She stopped beside Dean and placed her arms around his shoulders. "I didn't know you were back inside."

Dean stared up at his wife, and Gabriel's stomach twisted. The love they had for each other shone in their eyes so bright that it almost blinded him. Every time he saw that look between a man and a woman, he felt as if his heart had been broken once again.

He scooted his chair away from the table and stood up. His abrupt movement startled Gwen and Dean, and they both jerked their attention to him. "Is something wrong?" Dean asked.

Gabriel shook his head. "No. It's just been a long day. I think I'll head up to my room. I'll see you both in the morning. Good night."

"Good night," they called out, but he was already halfway to the stairs.

He hurried up the steps and strode down the upstairs hallway to his room. Once inside, he closed the door and stood there shaking all over. Seeing Gwen and Dean together tonight had brought back memories he thought he'd overcome. But when he least expected it, they resurfaced and kicked him in the gut.

He staggered across the room, sat down on the side of his bed and buried his face in his hands as the images he'd tried to repress came flooding back over him like a tidal wave.

No one could have asked for a more perfect day when he arrived at the church that afternoon ready to say the words that would make the woman he loved his wife. The pristine blue of the sky and the white clouds floating along only served to enhance the happiness he felt.

Soon he and Lana would be married and ready to start their life on the ranch his father had left him.

As the time grew nearer for the ceremony, he waited in a small room behind the church's choir loft. The first inkling he had that something wasn't right was when the appointed time arrived for the bridal march and nothing happened. A few minutes later the best man, who'd been his friend since childhood, walked into the room with a letter that had been delivered for him.

He opened it with shaking fingers, and the words on the page blurred as he began to read. She was sorry, she said, but she couldn't go through with the wedding. It would be unfair to him when she'd realized that she didn't love him. She apologized for the embarrassment and ended by saying that her parents would take care of letting the guests know and that she had left for New York.

At first he thought there was some mistake, but there wasn't. She was gone, and he'd lost the woman he loved. A few months later she returned to Texas to quietly marry his friend, the best man who'd delivered her letter. It seemed they'd been in love all along and had fought their attraction because of their respect for him. In the end, though, they couldn't overcome it. Soon after, he'd sold the ranch and applied to the FBI.

So here he was five years later, an agent with the FBI who lived out of an apartment in Memphis that he rarely saw. Lana and his former best friend had two children. Sometimes it didn't seem fair how his life had worked out. He hadn't done anything wrong, hadn't betrayed anyone's trust, and yet they were happy, while he was just going through the motions each day.

He didn't want to ever place himself in the position of being hurt like that again. He doubted if he would survive it a second time. Now he put all his energy into his job. There was nothing and no one else in his life, and he liked that just fine.

The only sad thing was that he would never have a woman look at him like Gwen Harwell looked at her husband tonight. The thought made his heart ache, but he shoved the feeling aside, refocusing on his assignment—taking care of Elizabeth Madison Kennedy, or Liz Madison, as she was calling herself. He would do everything to protect her, and in a few months he would take her safely back to Memphis to deliver testimony that would bring down a drug operation. Then he'd move on to the next assignment.

That was the only thing he needed to think about at the moment.

THREE

The morning sunshine felt warm on Liz's skin as she pushed the wheelbarrow out of the stable and headed toward the compost pile. She'd gone only a few feet when a voice behind her startled her.

"Good morning. I see you're already hard at work."

Her body stiffened in shock as she halted and jerked her head around to stare at Gabriel Decker, who was walking toward her. The big smile on his face turned to a frown when he saw her reaction. "I'm sorry. I didn't mean to scare you."

Liz took a deep breath to try to calm her racing heart and attempted a smile. "It's okay," she said. "I was pre-occupied and didn't hear you walk up."

His frown deepened, and he took a step closer. "Are you sure you're all right? You looked terrified when you turned around."

She nodded. "I'm fine."

His gaze moved over her face, and she had the feeling that he was uncertain whether she had been honest with him or not. There was no way she was going to tell him that she was used to being terrified. She'd lived that way in a safe house under protective custody for months until the FBI told her they were sending her to stay with a former police officer and his family at the other end of the state. After all she'd been through, she wasn't sure life would ever return to normal for her.

As she stared at Gabriel, she was once again struck by how handsome the man was, and this morning he looked especially so. Today he wore faded jeans and a chocolate-colored T-shirt that brought out the rich color of his eyes. He still had that bit of stubble on his face that made him blend in easily with the mountain men she'd met since arriving at Little Pigeon. She reminded herself that no matter how good-looking he was and how friendly he seemed, she had to be careful. She knew nothing about him, and she couldn't risk getting to know him.

She turned back to the wheelbarrow and gripped the handles. "Now if you'll excuse me, I'm mucking out the stalls, and I still have a lot of work to do."

"I'll help if you'd like," he said as she started to go.

She stopped again and turned back to him, her eyebrows lifted. "You're a paying guest, Mr. Decker. I don't think Dean would want you to be cleaning out stalls. It's hard work, and you're on vacation."

He grinned and speared her with his dark gaze. "I'm used to hard work, Liz, and I've cleaned out my share of stalls in the past. I'd be glad to help."

She hesitated for a moment and studied him. He seemed like a nice man, and although she didn't want to admit it, she had been lonely since she arrived. Dean and Gwen had been wonderful, but they had their own lives. She had tried not to interfere with that, which meant she'd kept to herself as much as possible. And really, what was the harm in letting him help? They were on the ranch property, with Dean and his employees all around. Even if Gabriel wasn't someone she could trust, surely he wouldn't be so blatant as to try to hurt her here.

After a moment, she smiled. "All right, Mr. Decker, I'd be happy to have the help."

His grin widened, and his eyes twinkled. "Gabriel, please. I thought we were on a first-name basis after I came to your aid yesterday."

She swallowed at the memory of the gun pressed to her head. "I appreciate what you did, more than I can ever tell you. But I'm trying to put that behind me, so I'd rather not talk about it anymore."

His eyes grew soft, and he tilted his head to one side. "I understand that. I won't bring it up again. Even though it wasn't an ideal meeting, I hope it will only be the beginning of our friendship."

Liz's face grew warm, and she looked down at her feet. "That sounds nice. I could use a friend. I haven't made any outside Gwen and Dean since I've been here."

"Then consider me the first."

She bit down on her lip and turned to put her hands back on the wheelbarrow. "Just let me dump this load at the compost pile, and I'll show you what needs to be done in the barn."

Before she could move, he was edging her out of the

way so he could wrap his fingers around the wheelbarrow handles. "I'll dump it. This looks like a heavy load."

Without waiting for her to respond, he pushed the wheelbarrow toward the compost pile and left her staring after him. She watched as he heaved the manure and stall shavings onto the rubbish heap and then walked back to her.

"That wasn't so bad."

She shook her head and laughed as she turned and headed back toward the barn. They'd taken only a few steps when Gabriel spoke again. "What's that building over there?"

Her gaze followed the direction he was pointing. "That's an old bunkhouse. I've been told that Dean's grandfather used it years ago when he had a lot of itinerant workers. It's been deserted for years. Dean turned it into a workshop and a supply shed for medicinal supplies for the horses. He keeps it locked all the time, but he's given me a key to it in case I need to get anything."

"I'd think he'd keep the medicines in the tack room where they'd be handy."

She shook her head. "No, the temperature can't be regulated in the barn."

"I see." By this time, they'd arrived back at the barn. "Okay, boss," he said, "show me what to do."

Once inside, she pointed out the stalls that still needed to be cleaned and motioned toward a room at the end of the barn alleyway. "Pitchforks are in there. Muck buckets are, too, but feel free to use the wheelbarrow."

He nodded. "I will."

She studied him as he turned and walked to the room where the tools were kept. His graceful movements told her that he was a man who was confident and relaxed in who he was. It also said something about him that he was a paying guest who didn't hesitate to offer his help with a job that most wouldn't consider doing. Still, there was something about him that she couldn't figure out. There were several young women staying at the ranch right now. They were much prettier than she was and wealthier, if their designer outfits were any indication. But for some reason he seemed to have singled her out for his attention. She couldn't understand why.

Shaking the thought from her head, she turned back to the stall in front of her and began to clean it. From time to time she and Gabriel crossed paths in the alleyway as they completed cleaning a stall and went to another. Each time their eyes met, he smiled, and she found herself responding to his friendly nature.

When they'd completed the job and put away the tools, they walked outside the barn and stared at the trail that led toward the mountains. Dean and Emmett, his foreman, rode toward them with a line of riders behind them.

"That's the early-morning trail ride coming back," Liz said. "They'll be hungry. I need to go get cleaned up so I can help Gwen and Shorty with lunch. Thanks for helping with the stalls."

She started to turn away, but he reached out and touched her arm. "It was my pleasure, Liz. I enjoyed the morning. What are you doing this afternoon?"

She shrugged. "I don't know. There are some more

guests arriving. I might have to help Gwen get the rooms ready. Why?"

"I picked up a brochure in the den and saw a picture of a creek near here. I think it's called Rattlesnake Creek. I was thinking that I might ride out there this afternoon. I wondered if you'd like to ride with me."

Liz paused for a moment before she replied. Her earlier concerns about Gabriel's attention to her returned, but they battled with her desire to make a friend and feel a little less lonely. "I don't know," she said. "Can I let you know after lunch?"

"Sure," he replied. "I talked to Dean before he left this morning, and he told me I could have Buttermilk about two o'clock. If you decide to go, meet me at the barn."

"I will."

She headed off toward the house but slowed down when she heard Gabriel call after her. "I really hope you'll decide to come."

Liz gave a small nod and continued walking. Right now she didn't know if she would go or not, but if she was really honest with herself, she'd admit that she wanted to. She wanted to find out more about Gabriel Decker and why he seemed interested in being with her. Maybe she'd take him up on the invitation after all.

By one o'clock the last guest had left the dining room, and Liz, Gwen and Shorty had the kitchen cleaned up. With the last pot stored away, Shorty took off the apron he wore and hung it on a peg beside the back door. "I need to pick up some things at the supermarket for the chuck wagon meal tomorrow night. Does either one of you need anything while I'm in town?"

Gwen and Liz both shook their heads.

"Be careful," Gwen said as the cook turned and walked toward the back door. "Those hairpin curves on the way into town scare me."

He grinned at her and nodded. "I'll watch out, Gwen. Don't you worry about me."

When he'd closed the door behind him, Gwen turned back to Liz. "Shorty worked for Dean's grandfather for years. So he's really like a member of the family, and I tend to worry about our family."

The concern on Gwen's face sent a warm glow through Liz. With both her parents dead, it had been a long time since she'd known what family really was about. Then she'd come to Little Pigeon Ranch and had seen it in the way Gwen and Dean treated each other, their daughter, Maggie, and all the people who worked for them. They had opened their home to her also and given her a safe haven during a traumatic time in her life.

She swallowed the lump she felt in her throat. "You make me feel like family, too, Gwen."

Gwen's eyes softened, and she grasped Liz's hand. "That's how we want you to feel, Liz. We're honored to have you in our home."

Tears sprang to her eyes, and she wiped at them. "Not many people would have done what you have for me. You didn't even know me, and yet you welcomed me with open arms, all the time knowing that you might be opening yourselves up to danger."

Gwen stared at her for a moment before she motioned toward a chair at the kitchen table. "Sit down, Liz, and let's have a glass of iced tea. I think you need a bit of cheering up after the busy day you've had."

Liz nodded and dropped down in the chair while Gwen poured their tea. When she'd filled the glasses, she set them on the table and took a seat. "Are you sleeping any better than you were when you first came?"

Liz shrugged. "Some nights I do, but last night wasn't very good."

"I'm sorry, but I guess that was to be expected after what happened. Have you thought about seeing a doctor? You could probably get a prescription for something to help you sleep."

She shook her head. "The doctor I saw in Memphis wanted to do that, but I don't want to be induced into sleep. I want to get back to the point that my mind is relaxed and I can drift off into peaceful dreams instead of the nightmares I have."

Gwen reached across the table and clasped her hand. "Liz, you'll get there. It just takes time."

Liz closed her eyes for a moment. "Every time I try to go to sleep, I remember what it was like that morning."

She paused, and Gwen leaned closer. "You know I told you anytime you wanted to talk, I'd listen. Maybe for your peace of mind you need to take me up on it."

"It's been hard for me to live with it, much less talk about it. But sometimes I think I'll scream with all the thoughts that run through my head. I think I do need to talk about it."

"Anytime you're ready, I'm here."

Liz sat still for a moment, the memories of the day that changed her life pouring through her mind. She had been wearing her favorite blouse, the one she had to throw away later because of all the bloodstains. And she remembered how Kathy had looked, her hair pulled back in a ponytail and her sunglasses propped on her head. For a moment she didn't know if she could bring herself to speak of what she'd seen. Then she inhaled, and the words tumbled out.

"It was a Friday, and I had taken the day off from work because I was leaving at lunchtime for a long weekend with my friend Kathy. We were going to a spa near Little Rock and were excited about getting away and spending a few days just being pampered. Kathy picked me up and said that she needed to stop at the mall before we left town and pick up a watch that she'd had repaired. When we got there, she pulled into the parking garage."

A sob choked her throat, and she swallowed. Gwen squeezed her hand tighter. "Are you sure you want to share this with me?"

She looked at Gwen through the tears that blurred her vision. "I need to talk about it. I told the police, but I haven't been able to tell anyone else. It brings back the terror that I felt that day."

Gwen nodded. "Okay."

Liz took a deep breath. "I told her I'd wait in the car since she would only be gone a few minutes. I wanted to check my email and texts. She laughed and said, 'You need to put everything out of your mind but the fun we're going to have, so I'm going to hide your phone this weekend.' Then she jumped out of the car and ran to the elevator."

She stopped for a moment, and Gwen said, "Go on."

"I don't know how long I sat there before I noticed a car pull in and stop two parking spaces down from me. A man got out. He was dressed casually and there wasn't anything special about him, but something about him drew my attention. Maybe it was the way he glanced around like he was looking for someone. Before he could move, a car drove up behind his and blocked it. Another man, this one well-dressed and looking like some kind of businessman, got out. They began to talk, and the first man I'd seen held out his hands like he was trying to explain something. Then he began to cry like he was begging. The man who'd blocked his car pulled out a gun and motioned for him to get down on his knees. I could hear the man pleading and crying as he dropped down. Then I heard shots."

"How horrible," Gwen said.

Liz bit her lip. "He turned around and started to leave, so I sank down in my seat hoping he wouldn't see me. That's when I heard the elevator door open."

Tears rolled down her face. "There were more gunshots, and I dropped down even lower in the seat. It seemed like an eternity before his car drove away. I sat up and looked around. That's when I saw Kathy lying close to the elevator. I ran to her, but she was already dead. I called 911, but I was screaming, so the dispatcher had a hard time understanding me."

Liz paused and closed her eyes. "There was blood everywhere. All over Kathy, all over me and on the floor."

"And then the police came." Gwen's tone told Liz she knew how the rest of the story went.

Liz sighed. "Yes, and they took me to the police station. They told me that the man who was murdered was a member of a drug ring that had been operating in the city and he'd been on the verge of agreeing to turn over evidence about his boss, who was the head of the organization. They wanted me to look at mug shots, and I must have gone through a hundred before I saw him—the shooter."

She shuddered remembering what it had been like when she saw the picture of the well-dressed man who'd pulled the trigger. "His name is Daniel Shaw, and he's the head of a crime family that the FBI has been after for years. They'd never been able to pin anything on him before. Now they had an eyewitness to murder, and they wanted me to testify."

"Which you agreed to do," Gwen said.

Liz nodded. "I didn't have a choice. I had to do it for Kathy. At the time, though, I didn't realize the danger I'd be in. They kept me at a safe house in the city at first, but when they noticed some suspicious men hanging around, they decided I'd be safer out of town. That's when the head of the Memphis office told me about Dean and how I'd be safe here until the trial. I've just been afraid that I was putting you and your family in danger."

Gwen shook her head. "Don't worry about that. Only Dean, Ben Whitman, Luke Conrad and I know your true identity. We'll do everything we can to keep you safe."

"Thank you, Gwen. I've tried to keep to myself a lot. I'm afraid I might let something slip, but it gets lonely. I miss my friends and my job in Memphis." Tears pooled in her eyes again. "Most of all I miss Kathy."

"Liz," Gwen began, her voice hesitant. "Maybe you need to make some friends. I know a young woman who is a trick rider at the Wild West show. She stayed with us when she first came here. She's married now to Ben's deputy Luke, and she's raising horses at their ranch. I think you'd like her a lot."

"A trick rider, huh? She sounds like an interesting person. Maybe you can introduce us."

"I'd be glad to."

Liz chewed on her lower lip for a second. "Actually, Gabriel Decker seems like he'd like to be friends. He asked me to go riding with him this afternoon."

The shadow of a frown flitted across Gwen's face before she straightened and cleared her throat. "I didn't think you were interested in getting to know him."

Liz shrugged. "I'm not, but I like to ride. It's more fun if you have someone else along."

Gwen studied her a moment. "So you're going to accept his invitation?"

Liz started to say no, but then she thought better of it. Maybe all he wanted was a bit of companionship, and she wanted to find out more about him. She knew it was risky to trust a stranger, but she couldn't make herself believe he wanted to hurt her. Not after the way he'd saved her the previous day or the way he'd spent all morning helping her. She'd stay on her guard, of course, but maybe it was all right to offer him this little bit of trust. Her decision made, she smiled.

"I am. I'll go find him now and tell him I've decided to go."

She pushed back from the table and strode to the door. Before she walked through it, she glanced back over her shoulder. Gwen still sat at the table, her brow furrowed and her eyes dark. For some reason Gwen didn't look too pleased with her decision. A flicker of apprehension stabbed at her stomach, and she swallowed. *No. I will not let fear rule my life*, she decided. Then she squared her shoulders and headed out the back door.

Gabriel glanced at his watch as he ambled up to the barn. It was still thirty minutes until the time he'd told Liz he'd meet her there, and he wondered if she'd come. Even though he'd made some progress in gaining her friendship this morning, she hadn't exactly jumped at the chance to go riding with him. He usually didn't have trouble relating to people, but then, witnessing a grisly murder could cause anyone to be wary of the people around her.

They'd had a good time this morning even if they were cleaning out stalls. He'd found he really missed the physical labor that it took to do a job like that, and he'd felt a sense of accomplishment when they'd finished. Now the horses had clean stalls and fresh shavings on the floor…until tomorrow. Then the job would have to be done again.

He walked into the barn and looked around in hopes that Liz had already gotten there, but he didn't see her. A noise in the far end of the alleyway attracted his attention, and he moved toward it. Dean stood inside the tack room cleaning a saddle. Gabriel stopped at the door and studied him briefly before he spoke.

"Hi, Dean. Need any help?"

"No, I'm fine. Are you going for that ride you asked me about this morning?"

Gabriel glanced at his watch. "Yeah. I'm hoping that Liz will go with me, but she hasn't shown up yet."

Dean came toward him, and Gabriel moved back so that Dean could step into the alleyway. "Where did you say you wanted to ride to?" Dean asked.

"Rattlesnake Creek. From what I saw on your brochure, it looks like a beautiful place."

"It is, and it's a nice ride up there."

A voice from behind startled Gabriel. "Do you need help saddling Buttermilk?"

He peered over his shoulder at the young man, perhaps nineteen or twenty years old, standing there. In his worn jeans, a Western shirt unbuttoned at the neck and boots, he looked like any other ranch hand Gabriel had seen since arriving. Dean turned and stared at him. "Bart, I thought you had the day off."

"That's right," Bart said, his eyes never leaving Gabriel's face. "Didn't have nothing to do. Thought I'd hang around here."

Dean looked back to Gabriel. "This is Bart Foster, one of our hands."

Gabriel stuck out his hand. "Gabriel Decker, Bart. Good to meet you.

Bart gave a curt nod as he shook Gabriel's hand, his steely gaze giving no sign of friendliness.

A strong vibe of suppressed anger radiated from the young man. His eyes held no sparkle, and the closed-off expression on his face indicated that he trusted no one. Gabriel had seen it on so many other faces of nameless prison inmates before. It was as if all hope had been sucked from their lives, to be replaced by despair. He wondered what this boy's story was.

"So should I get Buttermilk?" the ranch hand asked.

Gabriel shook his head. "Thanks for the offer, but I don't want to impose on you on your day off."

The boy shrugged. "No problem. She's in the corral. I'll round her up and throw a saddle on her."

As Bart turned to leave, the collar of his shirt opened farther to reveal the tattoo of a small fish on the side of his neck. Gabriel recognized it right away as a piranha, the symbol of a well-known gang that populated juvenile facilities. In places where the gang had a foothold, they thrived on putting fear in the inmates with the same fierceness that the tiny fish with razor-sharp teeth did in its victims. Even guards were afraid to stand against them.

Bart caught sight of Gabriel's eyes on his tattoo, and he lifted his chin challengingly. When Gabriel said nothing, Bart headed out the door. Gabriel frowned as he watched him go. When Bart stepped out of the barn, Gabriel glanced at Dean. "How long has Bart been working here?"

"A few weeks," Dean answered.

"What do you know about him?"

"Nothing really. He showed up here, a hungry kid who'd been drifting around the country. We get a lot of those through here, and I always try to help them out when I can. He's a hard worker. Keeps to himself. I can't help but believe he's carrying a lot of baggage. I don't think I've seen him smile since he's been here. Reminds me of how my life was at one time."

Gabriel hesitated for a moment before he said anything. Then he decided Dean had a right to know what he'd just discovered. "Dean, you need to keep a watch on him and make sure your family keeps their distance. That tattoo on his neck is the insignia of the Piranha Gang, who thrive in juvenile facilities. They're vicious and ruthless. Only trusted members are allowed to have the tattoo. So that means that at the very least, Bart was heavy into the gang at one time. It's possible he still is."

Dean's eyebrows arched. "Thanks for telling me, Gabriel. I'll keep an eye on him."

They stood there silently staring in the direction that Bart had gone. One thing Gabriel knew was that once a Piranha member was out of juvie, it didn't take long for the larger gangs in town to approach him. That could mean that Bart had already graduated to the next level and become a member of another gang. He wondered if Bart could now be tied to Shaw's organization. It seemed suspicious that he'd shown up right around the time of Liz's arrival. Yet on the other hand, if he was intent on attacking Liz, he wasn't acting very quickly. It was a puzzle.

Bart Foster could bear watching in the future, and he intended to do just that.

FOUR

Liz spotted Buttermilk saddled and ready to go as she approached the barn. She stopped and debated whether or not she really wanted to do this. She hadn't gone riding with another guest since she'd been here. Maybe she needed to turn around and go back to the house before Gabriel saw her. Then she could apologize later and blame the fact that she was exhausted after working so hard all morning.

She shook her head and frowned. There was no need to make excuses. If she didn't want to go, she didn't owe Gabriel Decker any explanation.

She turned to leave but faltered and worried her lip. The truth was that she wanted to go. She wanted to spend a few hours riding the trails that led into the mountains that ringed this valley, and she wanted to share the experience with another person who seemed friendly.

Before she could make a decision, Gabriel's voice called out to her. "Liz, I was about to give up on you."

She glanced over her shoulder and saw Gabriel leading Dandelion, the horse she'd been riding since coming here, from the barn. She was already saddled up, too. Liz hesitated only a moment before she took a deep breath and walked toward Gabriel.

"You didn't have to saddle Dandelion for me."

He smiled. "I didn't mind. I thought we could hit the trail as soon as you got here."

Dean walked out of the barn at that moment and raised a hand in greeting. "Liz, thanks for cleaning the stalls this morning. They look good."

"No need to thank me, Dean," she called out. "Mr. Decker did most of the work."

Dean's eyebrows rose, and he looked at Gabriel. "You didn't tell me that."

Gabriel waved his hand in dismissal. "She's too modest—she did more than her fair share. As for my part, it was no big deal. I was glad to do it." He smiled at Liz. "Besides, I enjoyed the company."

Liz's face flushed at his words. She knew it was just his way of being courteous but somehow it lifted her spirits. For the past few weeks she'd felt like she was in a vacuum. Although Dean and Gwen had been wonderful, she'd been away from her friends, her job and everything that was familiar to her. And on top of the fear and the worry, there was also the aching sadness she felt as she mourned her friend. All because she and Kathy had decided to stop at the mall on that horrible day. She doubted if her life would ever return to normal.

Without responding to Gabriel's comment, she took the reins from his hand and swung up onto Dandelion's back. When she was settled in the saddle, she looked down at Dean. "We should only be gone a few hours. I'll be back in time to help Gwen with dinner."

"Don't rush back for that. We can handle things. Just relax and have a good time. You've earned it."

She nodded and glanced around to see Gabriel mounted on Buttermilk. He grinned and swept his hand out in front of him. "Lead the way, Liz. I'll be right behind you."

She gave the horse a nudge, and they headed out onto the trail that led to Rattlesnake Creek. She'd ridden there once with Dean and knew that the ride would take them through some beautiful country. Familiar with the territory, Dandelion plodded along the trail.

The path grew wider, and Gabriel rode up beside her. She eyed him and noticed how relaxed in the saddle he looked. She'd seen some of the guests riding since she'd been here, and sometimes it was quite comical the way they seemed to be clinging to the saddle. Not Gabriel, though. He rode as if he'd been doing it all his life. Then she remembered he'd said he grew up on a ranch."

"I can tell you've ridden before. Where did you say you grew up?" she asked.

"Texas," he answered. "We had a ranch there. My parents left it to me, but I sold it about five years ago and left the area."

The way he clamped his lips together and grimaced told her that he wasn't about to say more about his early life. "So what do you do now?" she asked.

He didn't answer right away but then said, "I'm a consultant with a large organization that works with different agencies and businesses around the country to advise them on their operating practices. I'm taking a bit of a vacation for a while before I decide what I want to do next. What about you?"

"I'm a loan officer in a bank," she replied. "Not a very glamorous occupation, but I enjoy it."

"I'd think that would be difficult when you have to refuse to loan someone money."

She nodded. "It is, but it works the other way, too. Right before I came to Little Pigeon, I helped a young couple buy their first home. Their happiness and gratitude made me forget about those I'd seen disappointed."

He turned his head and stared at her. "I know the feeling when life hands you a disappointment but when you do something that helps someone out, it gives you a feeling that you've made a difference in another person's life."

A trace of bitterness laced his words, and she darted a glance at him. He stared straight ahead with his lips pursed as if he was lost in thought. Since she didn't understand what might have triggered his reaction, she cast around for a distraction.

Her gaze fell on some plants ahead. They hadn't been in bloom when she'd ridden here with Dean a few weeks earlier. She pointed to the brilliant display. "Look at that!"

A large group of Joe-Pye Weed plants stretched upward perhaps ten feet, and each of the stalks was covered with delicate lilac blooms. The sight took her breath away.

She pulled Dandelion to a stop and sat there drinking in the beauty. Gabriel halted Buttermilk beside her and rested his arm on the saddle horn as he gazed at the flowers. "What are they?"

"Joe-Pye Weed," she answered. "They blossom in the fall in the Smokies. Dean and Gwen had told me how beautiful they are, but they weren't in bloom the last time I rode this way."

He shifted his gaze to her. "You sound like you really enjoy looking at flowers."

"Oh, I do. When I was growing up, my mother always had flowers, and I would help with her garden." She sighed. "Now that I live in an apartment, I miss being able to have my own little spot to putter in. Maybe when I can go back home…"

She stopped before she said too much. She glanced at him and saw that he was studying her with a somber expression on his face. After a moment he swallowed and looked back at the plants. "That's certainly a breathtaking scene."

Relieved that he hadn't pushed her on what she'd meant to say, she reached in her pocket and pulled out her cell phone. "I think I'll get some pictures."

She fumbled with balancing the reins and the phone. Gabriel reached over and grasped the reins in his hand. "Let me hold these while you take the picture."

She released her grip, shot a quick smile his way and aimed the phone camera at the flowers that towered above them. Before she could take the picture, Dandelion raised her head and whinnied. Liz tightened her legs on either side of the horse and grabbed for the reins that Gabriel held. She had just wrapped her fingers around them when a gunshot split the air. The bullet kicked up dust a few feet in front of them.

Dandelion snorted and lunged toward the right side of the trail, away from Buttermilk. Liz's cell phone tumbled to the ground, and she tightened her grip on the reins in an effort to stay in the saddle.

"Liz!" Gabriel cried out, but she had no time to look at him.

She gritted her teeth and pulled back on the left rein. Dandelion's head turned in that direction as if they were going in a circle. Then a second shot hit the ground in front of them, and with a loud whinny the horse jerked her head, reared up on her back legs and pawed at the air.

Liz tried to keep hold of the reins, but when they slipped from her hands, she grabbed the saddle horn in an attempt to stay seated. At the sound of a third shot, Dandelion surged forward. Liz tightened her legs on either side of the horse to keep from being thrown, but it was no use. Dandelion bucked once more, and Liz felt herself falling.

She screamed just before darkness consumed her.

It all happened so fast Gabriel didn't have time to react. One minute Liz was taking a picture, and the next, bullets were flying. He heard the crack of the rifle and saw the dust kick up. His first thought was to grab for Liz, but Buttermilk lunged away in the wrong direction. She was as terrified as Dandelion. The second and third shots sent the horses into a panic.

He yanked on Buttermilk's reins as he watched in horror as Liz fell from the saddle to the ground. As soon as Dandelion was free of her rider, she took off running and disappeared down the trail. Gabriel jumped off his horse, which gave a loud whinny and then galloped off after Dandelion.

There was no time to worry about the horses. He pulled his gun from its holster, aimed into the forest where the shots had come from and fired as he ran toward Liz. When he reached her, he grabbed her arm and dragged her across the trail into the trees opposite the shooter. Two more shots hit on either side of him as he pulled her to the shelter of the forest, and he returned the fire.

When they were in the relative safety of the woods, he released his hold on Liz, pulled off his jacket and placed it under her head. His gaze raked her from head to foot. He didn't see any injuries, but she must have hit her head when she fell or she wouldn't be unconscious. She could have serious internal injuries. He slipped his fingers into her hair and felt around her scalp but found nothing that seemed out of the ordinary.

He sat back on his heels, closed his eyes and pressed his lips together. He couldn't believe he'd been so careless in bringing Liz out here. Instead of convincing her to go riding with him, he should have thought up ways to gain her trust without leaving the ranch. He'd only begun his assignment to protect her yesterday, and she'd already had two incidents that reeked of Daniel Shaw's gang.

Now she lay injured in a forest, someone was out there shooting at them and there was no backup anywhere close by. The more he thought about it, though, the stranger it seemed. If the gunman was a hit man for Daniel Shaw, why were the shots aimed at the trail and not them? From such a short distance the gunman shouldn't have had any trouble hitting them if that's what he'd intended. Maybe this had been a warning, an attack designed to scare Liz and keep her from testifying.

He glanced at his watch and realized it had been at least five minutes since the last shot. Maybe whoever was out there had gone. Only one way to find out. He crawled to the edge of the tree line and peered across the trail. He saw no movement. Taking a deep breath, he raised his gun and shot into the forest opposite them. There was no answering gunfire. He shot once more. When nothing happened, he crawled back to Liz. She still hadn't moved.

He pulled his cell phone from his pocket and punched in Dean's number. He answered right away. "Hello."

"Dean, we've had a problem. Someone took a few shots at us, and Liz was thrown. The horses have run off, and we're stranded. Can you come get us?"

Dean gasped. "Are you both all right?"

"I'm okay, but Liz is unconscious. You're going to need an ATV to get her. There's no way we can get her on a horse, and I wouldn't want to risk potentially aggravating any injuries she might have, anyway."

"What about the shooter?"

"I think he's gone, but be careful. He could be waiting until we come out of hiding."

"Emmett and I will be right there. Where are you?"

Gabriel searched for a landmark, and he thought of the flowers. "We are off the trail next to a big stand of Joe-Pye Weed. They're really tall and have lilac blooms. You can't miss them."

"I know the place. Hang in there," Dean said. "We're on our way."

Gabriel disconnected the call, slipped the phone back in his pocket and looked down at Liz. A wince flitted across her face, and she groaned. He bent closer. "Liz, can you hear me?"

Another groan, and her eyes blinked open. She squinted as if trying to focus and then stared up at him. "Gabriel, what happened?"

"You had a fall from your horse. Just lie still. Dean is on his way to get us."

She frowned and tried to push herself up, but Gabriel grabbed her shoulders and eased her back to the ground. "Don't move until Dean gets here. I don't think you have any injuries, but we won't know for sure until you're checked out by a doctor."

She rubbed her forehead with her hand and furrowed her brow. "I fell? I've never done that before. Something must have…" Her voice trailed off, and her lips began to tremble. "Gunshots. I remember gunshots hitting the ground in front of Dandelion, and then the horse reared."

He nodded. "Yes, but I think the shooter is gone now."

Her eyes grew wide, and she pushed up into a sitting position. "Oh, Gabriel, do you think…"

She bit down on her lip and stopped talking. From the fear in her eyes he could almost read her thoughts. There had been the attack yesterday in the movie parking lot, and today someone had shot at her. She had to be wondering if the two incidents had anything to do with her testimony.

But he wasn't supposed to know about that, so he'd have to play dumb. "Think what?" he asked.

Her face turned ashen, and beads of sweat popped up on her forehead. With a groan she jumped to her feet and let her frightened gaze dart about the forest. Then she took a step back from him and fixed him with a questioning look. "I don't get it."

"Liz, sit down. You've had a fall." He moved toward her, but she shook her head and backed away.

"I've been attacked two days in a row. Yesterday you just happened to be coming out of the movie when I needed help. Today you convince me to go riding with you, and someone shoots at me. It's quite a coincidence that you were there both times."

He took another step toward her, but she retreated even farther. "Don't come any nearer," she said. "If you were telling the truth, Dean should be here any minute."

He sighed. "Of course I was telling you the truth. Why wouldn't I?"

She frowned. "I don't know, but I'm not an idiot. I knew from the first moment I saw you that something wasn't right. You're too intent on getting close to me." She continued backing away, and she gasped when she found herself with her back against a tree.

His heart lurched at the fear he saw in her eyes, and he moved closer. "Liz, you're being unreasonable."

Tears filled her eyes, and one rolled down her cheek. "Who are you?" she screamed. "What do you want with me?"

Gabriel sighed and raked his hand through his hair. He should have known Liz would see through him. She had run to the mountains to try to save her life, and she was scared and afraid to trust anyone. He couldn't blame her. Honestly, he was glad she was wary. If she was too trusting, it would put her in danger. But if she kept doubting him, he wouldn't be able to do his job. Her safety was the most important thing, which meant that now he was going to have to tell her the truth.

"Okay, I guess you deserve an explanation. I would be skittish, too, if I'd been through what you have."

Her eyes widened. "Wh-what do you mean?"

"I know it was hard seeing your friend killed, and it was even harder agreeing to testify. That took a lot of courage. Not many people would do that."

Her face looked as if all the blood had left her body. "Y-you know about that? But how?"

He hesitated a moment before he spoke. "I know because I'm an FBI agent, sent here undercover to protect you."

Her forehead wrinkled, and she shook her head. "I don't understand."

"We thought that if we got you out of Memphis, we could keep you safe until Shaw's trial. Then one of our informants told us that a contract had been placed on your life, that there was a hit man trying to track you down. My boss sent me to protect you until I can return you safely to Memphis."

"A contract?" Her voice quivered as she spoke. "Do Dean and Gwen know?"

"Yes."

"Then why did they let me go to the movies yesterday?"

"Your location has been very well protected—we didn't have any reason to believe that anyone had succeeded in finding you. Besides, they knew I was going to be there, so they felt okay about it. Turns out we should have been more concerned. I'm sorry about today. I kept after you to go riding, and you could have been killed."

She didn't reply for a second, studying him. "How long will you be here?"

"Until the trial date. There's another agent coming today to help. Her name is Andrea Cauthorn. We'll do everything we can to make sure you're safe. I know you haven't felt at ease with me, but you're going to have to get over that. If someone knows you're here, then it's not safe for you to be alone, even on the ranch. From now until I deliver you to the court to testify, I'm going to stick to you like glue."

She directed a frosty gaze at him. "At least now you won't have to play on my loneliness to spend time with me. I won't delude myself anymore by thinking maybe I've found a friend I can enjoy doing things with. I'll know it's just a job with you, not a real attempt at friendship."

"That's not true, Liz," he said. "I like you. I do want to be your friend, but most of all, I want you to be safe. I did what I thought was best in keeping my identity a secret. Please try to understand. I'm not your enemy. I'm here to protect you."

Her eyes narrowed, and she started to say something but was interrupted by the sound of a voice on the trail. "Liz! Gabriel! Where are you?"

"That's Dean," he said. "Can you walk back to the trail, or do I need to carry you?"

He reached out as if to help her, and she raised her hands to ward him off, then let them drift to her sides. "No, thank you. I can do it by myself."

His heart sank at the cold glare she leveled at him. He really had liked the time they'd spent together today, and he regretted that she might not feel as relaxed with him again. He watched her turn and walk toward the trail. After a moment he took a deep breath and followed her.

He hoped he hadn't ruined everything by blowing his cover, but she was bound to find out sooner or later. That had never bothered him before on other cases. Each one was just a job to be done so he could move on to the next one. In this case, it was his responsibility to see that Daniel Shaw went to prison. He wasn't here to make friends with a witness. He just had to protect her until she could testify in court. When she'd done that, he would be through with this case and turn his attention to the next.

That's the way he'd always worked, and that's what he intended this time. It was the way he rolled, and he wasn't about to change now.

FIVE

An hour later, Liz sat at the kitchen table with Gwen, Dean and Gabriel drinking a cup of coffee. A heavy silence hung over the room, and for the first time since coming to the ranch, Liz felt uncomfortable. She still couldn't believe that Dean and Gwen had known that Gabriel was an FBI agent and hadn't told her. She picked up her mug and stared into the hot liquid, then took a sip.

From time to time Liz glanced at Gabriel, but they really hadn't had a chance to talk since they'd returned to the ranch. She was still trying to figure out how she really felt about the things Gabriel had said.

Gwen, who sat in the chair next to her, reached over and wrapped her fingers around Liz's arm. "I wish you'd reconsider and let us take you to the emergency room just to make sure that you don't have any internal injuries."

Liz shook her head. "I'm okay. I've fallen off horses before. I may be a little sore in the morning and will probably have a few bruises, but that's all."

She looked across the table at Dean and swallowed at the troubled expression on his face. "I know right now you feel like we should have been more forthcoming with you, but we did what the head of the Memphis FBI office wanted. He was afraid you'd take off and disappear if you knew how dangerous the case had gotten. We felt you'd be safe here. Maybe we were naive to think that."

Liz composed herself and sat up straight in her chair. "I'm not angry at any of you. I'm angrier with myself for not realizing it sooner. I feel like I should have known. If I had, I could have made some different choices. I wouldn't have gone to the movie yesterday." She cut her eyes around to stare at Gabriel. "And I wouldn't have made the mistake of going riding with you today."

Other than a quick blink of his eyes, Liz couldn't tell her words had affected him at all. "It wasn't your mistake, Liz. It was mine. I should have known better. We won't let that happen again."

She set her cup down and turned to face him. "So now that I know who you really are, how are we going to handle this? Do we need to leave, now that Shaw's people know where I am? Will I be relocated to somewhere new?"

"Not at this time," Gabriel confirmed, having just gotten off the phone with Bill and discussed this very question. "We're looking into other options of places where you can go, but in the meantime, we feel you're safer here, where you have plenty of people looking out for you."

"Will you spend every waking minute with me? Will we be joined at the hip, so to speak?"

His mouth quirked a bit, but he didn't laugh. "No.

You'll just go about life as usual, but from now on you'll stick close to the ranch and I'll be here with you. Or... I told you there's another agent coming today. You may find you like her better than you do me and want her to be with you most of the time."

Liz wondered what this new agent would be like. At least they'd be able to be honest with each other from the start—there'd be no need for pretense now that she knew why the agents were there.

"I'm sure both of you are good agents. I admit I was angry at first when you told me who you were, but that's because I was left in the dark while the people closest to me knew. You don't have to worry about me causing any problems. Just do your job and offer me protection—I'll be happy with that."

A small smile pulled at Gabriel's lips. "I'm relieved to hear you say that. I thought for a moment there I might have to tell Bill Diamond that you disliked me so much I needed to be taken off the case."

"No, I won't do that." She pushed back from the table and stood. "Now, I'm going to excuse myself and go upstairs. I think I could use a nap before dinner. I'll be back down to help you when it's time to serve, Gwen."

Gwen shook her head. "No, you rest. Shorty and I can handle the dinner guests."

"All right. Then I'll see you later." She turned to leave but stopped at the door leading into the dining room and looked back at Gabriel. "By the way, what's the other agent's name again?"

"Andrea Cauthorn. She should be arriving soon."

Liz nodded and left the room. She had just reached

the stairs and was about to go up to her room when the front door opened. A woman dressed in a black pantsuit walked in. Her dark hair was pulled back in a severe bun that offered a sharp contrast to her flawless porcelain skin. Liz didn't think she'd ever seen a woman with such a beautiful complexion.

A smile brightened her eyes as she set down an overnight bag she was carrying and stuck out her hand. "I'm Andrea Cauthorn. I'm checking in."

Liz shook the woman's hand and let her gaze drift over her. "And I'm your assignment," she said. "Liz Madison."

Andrea's eyebrows arched. "You know who I am?" she asked.

"Yes. Gabriel told me you'd be coming to help keep an eye on me. I'll try not to give you any problems while you're here. I know you and Gabriel are here to help me."

Andrea's eyes widened in surprise, and then her gaze drifted down the hallway and to the rooms on either side. "Where is Gabriel? I expected him to be close by."

"He's in the kitchen with Gwen and Dean." Liz pointed in the direction. "Follow this hallway, and you can't miss it. Gwen will get you checked in and settled in your room. Now, if you'll excuse me, I was on my way upstairs. I'll see you later."

She started to step around Andrea, but the agent reached out and placed a hand on Liz's arm. Liz glanced up at Andrea, who had her head tilted to one side and was studying her. "Why do I get the impression that you're not happy about something?"

Liz sighed. "I'm still trying to recover from the fact that the FBI thought it necessary to send two agents here to protect me from a threat they didn't share with me. I found out this afternoon who Gabriel is and that Dean and Gwen knew. I guess I felt like I'd been blindsided. I don't want anything hidden from me concerning this case. If I'm in danger, I think I should know it so that I can help avoid it if possible."

"All we want to do is protect you, Liz. You sound as though something might have happened to get you upset. What was it?"

"I'm sure Gabriel will tell you all about it." She paused and took a deep breath. "So just let me say thank you for being willing to take on this assignment, and I'll try to cooperate with you."

Andrea smiled. "That's good to know. We have a job to do, and it will make things go easier if we can be friends."

Liz doubted that was possible. If things were different and she had met Andrea and Gabriel at a party in Memphis or at church, they might have been able to develop a friendship. But the reality was that they hadn't come here to make friends with her. She was just one in a long list of victims that they worked with every day. She had no doubt that they'd be kind to her, but they had to stay focused and remain emotionally detached, so cordial respect was likely as far as it would ever go.

When she had learned earlier that Gabriel was an undercover agent, she'd felt betrayed. He, like so many others in her life, had hidden the truth from her.

People had been keeping secrets from her all her life.

It wasn't until after her parents' deaths in a car crash that she found papers in their safe-deposit box finalizing her adoption. All those years, and they'd never told her. Then two years ago she'd given her boyfriend a huge chunk of her inheritance to help him start a business. She discovered later the money had gone to cover gambling debts.

So she'd had her share of secrets being kept from her by people she'd trusted in the past, and she wasn't about to set herself up to have the same thing happen again. Since she had no control over whether or not people chose to keep things from her, she'd just have to be a lot choosier in who she trusted. There would be no friendship with Gabriel or Andrea. They were here for the moment, and when the trial was over, they'd be gone.

So for the time being she'd put on her best game face and try to cooperate. She owed it to Kathy to stay alive so she could testify against her killer. When the trial was over, she had no idea what she'd do. But right now she was going to take it one day at a time and pray that Gabriel and Andrea could help keep her and all the people she'd come to love at Little Pigeon safe.

Gabriel stared at the kitchen door as it closed behind Liz. Liz had said if they did their jobs and protected her, she would be happy. Somehow he didn't think she would be. The way her voice cracked when she said it and the way she clenched her hands at her sides told him she was unhappy right now. He rose from his chair and took two steps to follow her, then stopped.

He turned to face Gwen and Dean, who'd gotten to their feet. "This is all my fault," he said. "I'm sorry."

Dean frowned. "For what?"

"Liz is angry with all of us because of the secret I asked you to keep. You don't deserve it after all you've done for her."

Gwen shook her head. "She's still trying to wrap her head around all of it. She'll be all right. I don't think we need to do anything differently. We'll just continue to be her friend and keep our eyes open."

Gabriel rubbed the back of his neck and exhaled heavily. "It doesn't sound like she wants any kind of friendship with me. But maybe that's just as well. She doesn't need to become too attached to me. When this case is over, we'll probably never see each other again."

Dean nodded. "I understand. You have to keep your relationship with the people you protect purely professional. You start to lose your edge when you begin to care too much."

Gwen laughed and poked him in the ribs with her elbow. "If you'd done that when I was the one needing your protection as a police officer, we wouldn't be married today."

Dean laughed, too, and reached over and kissed his wife on the cheek. "Well, there are exceptions to every rule."

Gabriel had never seen a couple who seemed so at ease with one another and so in love. That's how he'd thought his life would turn out, but it hadn't. He doubted it ever would. He cleared his throat and started to tell them he'd see them later when the kitchen door opened.

Andrea walked in, stopped and placed her hands on her hips.

A smile pulled at her lips. "Shame on you, Gabriel. I see you've already managed to mess things up, as usual."

He cocked an eyebrow and stared at Andrea. "What's that supposed to mean?"

She laughed. "I met Liz in the hallway, and I could tell she wasn't happy about finding out she had two agents assigned to watch over her. It's almost like she thought we were babysitters."

"Well, we both know that's not the case, especially since she's had two attempts on her life since I've been here."

Andrea's eyes grew wide. "What happened?"

For the next few minutes he told Andrea about the mugging in the parking lot and the shooter in the trail. When he finished, he glanced from her to Dean and Gwen, who had stood silently while he was speaking. "So we have a very real threat here. Liz's location has been revealed, which means her life is in danger. We're going to have to make sure nothing happens to her. She needs somebody with her at all times."

Andrea nodded, looking somber. "You're right, Gabriel. How do you want to handle this?"

He shook his head. "It's not going to be easy. She's unhappy with us, but she's also afraid. Anything she says or does to discourage us has to be ignored. We have to keep in mind that the most important thing is that she's protected."

Andrea nodded. "I agree."

He took a deep breath. "I don't think she's gonna want to give up her chores around here, and that's good. The busier she stays, the less time she'll have to worry." He looked at Andrea. "I know you don't like horses, so I'll stay with her while she's cleaning out stalls or taking care of the horses in the mornings. Andrea, you can take over when she's here in the house and for the afternoon, and we can both keep an eye on her at dinner and the evening. How's that?"

"Suits me," Andrea said. "I'm glad you volunteered for stable duty. I don't think I'm cut out for that."

Gwen approached Andrea. "If that's all decided, I'll help you get settled in your room. Where did you park your car?"

"In the circle drive in front of the house."

"If you'll give Dean your car keys, he'll get your luggage and move your car to our parking area."

Andrea handed Dean her keys and then followed Gwen from the room. After they'd left, Dean turned to him, but before he could speak, his phone rang. He pulled it from his pocket and stared at the caller ID. "It's Ben Whitman."

He raised the phone to his ear. "Ben? What's going on?" His face suddenly grew pale, and he glanced at Gabriel. "Wait a minute, Ben. Gabriel is here with me. I'm going to put you on speaker."

"What is it?" Gabriel whispered.

Dean didn't answer as he switched the call. "Okay, go on."

"I wanted to let you know," Ben said, "that the name of Liz's attacker from the theater parking lot is Gene

Curtis. His prints were in the system because he's been in and out of jail since he was seventeen."

"Any known ties to Daniel Shaw?" Gabriel asked.

"He's a suspected hit man for the organization, but nobody's ever been able to prove it."

Dean and Gabriel let out long sighs at the same time. "Since you have him in custody, maybe you can get him to talk."

"That's going to be hard to do."

Gabriel frowned. "Why?"

"Because Deputy Conrad and I had to go to Knoxville this morning. While we were gone, Curtis's lawyer managed to get a bail hearing for him, and the judge released him."

Gabriel's mouth dropped open. "But how could he do that? There were charges of assault with a deadly weapon and attempted kidnapping."

"Because there was no arrest report. It had conveniently disappeared from our files. With no charges and the two arresting officers out of town, the judge gave him bail."

"What time was that?" Gabriel asked.

"About ten o'clock."

The muscle in Gabriel's jaw flexed at the answer. That meant that Curtis was out of jail when he and Liz had been ambushed. "Somebody took some shots at Liz and me up close to Rattlesnake Creek a little after two this afternoon. Curtis would have had plenty of time to get to the ranch and keep a lookout for us."

"Yeah, but to do that, he would've had to know where you'd be, which indicates that if it was him, he had an accomplice," Ben answered. "Whoever shot at the two of you, be careful. Stay close to the ranch, and we'll do everything we can to find this guy."

"We will, Ben. Thanks for letting us know."

Dean disconnected the call, and the two of them stared at each other for a moment before Gabriel spoke. "Can you believe that?"

Dean shook his head. "There must be a mole in Ben's office. Somebody was paid to make that arrest record disappear."

Gabriel nodded. "I agree. And also, Ben may be right about Curtis having an accomplice. The security on Liz just got a bit tighter."

"What do you mean?" Gabriel froze at the sound of Liz's voice.

He turned to see her standing in the doorway, and he could tell from the look on her face she'd heard what he'd said. Dean stared down at the keys in his hand and cleared his throat. "I think I'll go get Andrea's luggage. I'll let you tell Liz what has happened."

Liz came farther into the room as Dean walked past her. When he was gone, she took another step toward him. "What's going on, Gabriel?"

He pulled a chair out from the table and motioned her toward it. "Have a seat, and I'll tell you."

She sank down in the chair, and he took the one across from her. Then he related the conversation he and Dean had just had with Sheriff Whitman. Her chin trembled while he spoke, and her eyes took on a misty sheen. He could tell she was barely holding it together.

She had clasped her hands in front of her on the table,

and her knuckles were white. As he finished speaking, he reached across and covered her hands with his. "Don't worry, Liz. We're not going to let anything happen to you."

A tear rolled from the corner of her eye and made a trail down her cheek. He'd seen other victims he worked with cry at bad news, but somehow this was different. He'd been briefed on Liz's background, and he knew the woman who was killed was her best friend. Both parents were dead, and there were no siblings. She had to feel so alone.

She looked down at his hands on hers and stared at them for a moment before she raised her head and looked into his eyes. "I know you and Andrea will do your job, and I really appreciate it even if I did sound ungrateful earlier. I have to stay safe for Kathy's sake. I owe it to her to put her killer behind bars, so I'll do whatever you tell me to."

He smiled and squeezed her hand. "Good. We're going to get through the next few weeks, and then I'm going to deliver you back to Memphis. I'll stay close until you testify. When the jury finds Daniel Shaw guilty and puts him away for good, I'll take you out to dinner at one of the finest restaurants in Memphis."

She pulled her hands away from his and folded them in her lap. "Let's get one thing straight before we go any further. I don't want you saying things to me that you think I want to hear just because you think I need some kind of motivation to get me through the next few weeks. We both know I'm just your latest assignment. When this is over, you'll move on to the next victim and won't give me another thought. So what I'm saying is, you don't need to promise things you don't intend to deliver."

Her words shocked him, and he sat back in his chair. "Liz, I would never lie to you."

She pushed back from the table, stood and stared at him. "Then why do I feel like you did that when you hid the truth about who you really are from me?" She glanced at her watch. "Now I need to go to the barn and check on the horses. I'll see you at dinner."

He sat there stunned for a few minutes after she walked out the back door. Her words stung, and he raked his hand through his hair. He hadn't meant to upset her. In fact, he'd been speaking honestly when he'd said he would like to take her out to dinner when this was all over.

She was right to turn him down—it was inappropriate for him to make her promises like that. It was even more inappropriate that he still wanted to keep it.

For some reason ever since he'd seen her pressed against the door of her car with a gun to her head, he'd felt more protective than he ever had before. Maybe it was because of the danger surrounding her, or maybe it was because of the vulnerable look in her eyes that told him she was struggling to be brave in the face of imminent danger.

Whatever the reason, she wasn't going to make him feel guilty for doing his job. Suddenly his eyes grew wide. What was the matter with him? He was sitting at the kitchen table nursing his hurt feelings while Liz had gone to the barn alone. He jumped up and rushed out the back door.

He frowned when he didn't see Liz. She hadn't had time to get to the barn, but she was nowhere in sight. A flash of color caught his eye, and he saw her at the door of the workshop where all medications were stored. He watched as she pulled a key ring from her pocket and inserted a key into the door's padlock. She appeared to be on a mission and didn't look behind her even to close the door.

He hesitated briefly, then followed her. She probably wouldn't be happy to see him, but he needed to keep an eye on her. He'd wait out here and follow her back to the barn when she came out.

At that moment Bart Foster walked from behind the building, stopped and looked around. Gabriel slipped behind a tree and watched as Bart's gaze drifted past him. He wondered what Bart could be up to. As he watched, his suspicions of Bart grew. This guy was a known gang member from juvie. Maybe he was the accomplice Ben suspected Gene Curtis of having.

Bart surveyed his surroundings once more before he eased over to the workshop's open door, glanced over his shoulder again and slipped inside. The door closed behind him.

Gabriel bolted from behind the tree and ran as fast as he could across the hard ground. He had to get to Liz before Bart had a chance to hurt her.

SIX

The bottle Liz was holding crashed to the floor and shattered as the door to the workshop burst open. Her mouth gaped open as Gabriel rushed into the room. "What's going on?" she cried. "You scared me to death."

He hurried toward her and stopped in front of her. "Are you all right?"

"Well, I was until you barreled through the door and scared the living daylights out of me. What's the matter?"

He cast a wild-eyed look all around him. "I saw Bart Foster come in here. Where is he?"

"I'm right here."

Bart's voice came from across the room, and Gabriel swiveled to see him entering from another room. He held several bottles in his hands. Gabriel glanced back at Liz, and her eyes narrowed. "Bart saw me walk in here, and he came to help me out. He knows I have trouble sometimes getting what I need off the top shelf. What did you think? That he was up to something else?"

Gabriel's face flushed, and he shook his head. "I—I didn't know. I thought you might need…"

"Some protection?" she finished for him. "In this instance, I don't." She walked over to Bart and took the bottles from his hands. "Thank you for your help, Bart. I appreciate it."

A sullen expression crossed Bart's face as he glared at Gabriel for a moment before he turned back to Liz. "Then I'll get on back to the bunkhouse, Miss Madison."

Liz smiled. "I asked you to call me Liz."

Bart gave a curt nod and cut his eyes back to Gabriel. "I'll try to remember to do that."

He turned and walked toward the door, but Liz called after him. "Don't forget. This is our night for the checkers game. I'll have the table set up on the front porch about seven o'clock. Will you be there?"

Bart paused, eyed Gabriel once more and then nodded. "I'll see you then."

When Bart had left, Liz turned back to Gabriel. "Now are you going to tell me what that was all about?"

"I was just doing my job, Liz."

"By rushing in here like a madman? Bart has helped me a lot of times before today, and he's never given me any reason to question his motives."

He reached out and touched her arm. "Liz, I have to be suspicious of everybody. You seemed awfully friendly with that boy. Do you think that's wise?"

Her eyes widened, and she stared at him. "Why wouldn't it be?"

His Adam's apple bobbed, and he frowned as if trying to decide what to say. "Well, I mean…what do you know about Bart Foster?"

She shrugged. "Nothing really. He hasn't told me much. I can tell, though, that he hasn't had an easy life. I think it's admirable the way he's managed to get on the right track, working here."

"Maybe you should rethink that, Liz. Did you see the tattoo on his neck?"

"Yes. What about it?"

"Any guy who has a Piranha tattoo on his neck is bad news."

Liz stared at him, then shook her head. "Bart came to Little Pigeon a few days after I did, and neither of us had friends here. I think we kind of gravitated toward each other. I asked him about the tattoo, and he told me all about it."

"So you know the Piranhas are a vicious gang?"

"Yes, and he told me that he only let them tattoo him because he was scared. He knew if he didn't accept the invitation to join them, they would target him and he might not leave juvie alive. Now he has to wear that disgusting mark on his neck. But at least it's on the outside." She paused a moment, and when she spoke again, her voice rose with each word until her body was shaking. "I've known lots of people who had much worse branded on their souls. Even a good-looking and well-dressed person can commit a heinous crime without batting an eye. When they do, it becomes evident that there's some kind of evil living in that person."

"Liz, I'm sorry if I upset you. I was only trying to…"

She held up her hand to stop him. "I know you thought you were protecting me, but you can't assume the worst about every person who comes in contact with me. I learned a long time ago not to judge a person by what you see. Only God can see the heart, and I try to let God's eyes look through me to another person."

He studied her carefully. "I see that I really have upset you. I didn't mean to do that. All I want to do is protect you. I may not always do it the way you think I should, but I'll do everything I can to keep you safe. I guess I've become too cynical where other people are concerned. In my experience, you have to be careful when you put your trust in someone. It's impossible to know what ulterior motives may be in another person's mind."

Liz frowned. "That is a pessimistic way to approach life. People may have their own motives, but that doesn't mean they deserve to be treated with distrust and suspicion instead of grace."

"Yeah, well," he said, "I don't see much evidence of grace in my work. How can God allow bad things like that to happen? Where was He when your friend Kathy was dying in that parking garage?"

"I don't understand why Kathy died. She was one of the best people I've ever known. She was the kind of person who would stop on the road and pick up stray animals. Sometimes her house looked like a hospital for dogs and cats. She was my best friend, and I miss her terribly." She paused for a moment to swallow. "You want to know where God was that day? He was there. He watched over Kathy while she was dying, and He protected me, cowering in the car."

Her heart pricked at the flicker of pain she saw flash in his eyes. Whatever had happened to him in his past had erected a barrier in his life that kept everybody and everything at bay. It might keep out people who wanted to hurt him—but it kept out love and happiness, too. A stab of remorse for what he'd chosen to ignore in life saddened her.

After a moment, she sighed. "Gabriel, I can tell something has caused you a lot of hurt, and I'm sorry about that. I have had my own share of troubles, too, and I know how much it hurts. But we can't give up hope. We have to realize that we have no control over what happens to us, but God does. That's the only way I can face each day."

Gabriel put his hands in his pockets and rocked back on his heels. "I'm glad it works for you."

"It can for you, too, but only you can make that choice." She glanced down at the bottles, the cellophane and the cloth wraps in her hands. "I'd better get back to the stable. One of the horses seems to have some stiffness in his leg. I need to rub him down, wrap the area in cellophane and cover it with this cotton wrap. Do you want to come with me?"

He nodded and followed her from the workshop. As they walked toward the barn, a horse whinnied in the corral, and they both glanced that way. Dandelion and Buttermilk stood looking over the fence at them.

Gabriel laughed. "Do you think those two are ashamed at how they treated us today?"

She shook her head. "I doubt it. If anything, they're probably annoyed with us for putting them in that position. If you want to get back in their good graces, you can pick up a couple apples from the barrel inside the barn and give them each one. Bribery works every time."

He laughed again as they stepped inside the barn, and she realized for the first time how his eyes twinkled when he laughed. Gabriel Decker appeared to have many layers to his personality, and she found herself wishing that they'd met somewhere else instead of her being his assignment. She would like to help him explore whatever had caused him to be so cynical because she thought there was a man underneath who was worth getting to know.

Gabriel watched as Liz walked down the alleyway of the barn, her back straight and her head high, and thought about the things she'd said to him. How had a conversation about something like gang tattoos morphed into what closely resembled an argument about faith?

Her comments about seeing people through God's eyes had come as a blow. No one had told him she was a believer. Maybe that's what had enabled her to live with what she saw that day and gave her the strength to face a murderer in court. It didn't matter what had helped her cope—his job was to see that she got to court safely to give her testimony.

Shaking his head, he picked up two apples from the barrel and ambled out the barn door to the corral fence. He leaned against it as he studied the two horses that had left Liz and him stranded earlier. Buttermilk eyed him a few seconds before he walked over and stood facing Gabriel.

Gabriel held out the apple. Buttermilk gave a whinny and closed his teeth around the treat. Then he sauntered back across the corral.

"Do you have no loyalty?" Gabriel called out in mock despair. "Do you only like me for what I can give you?"

"My, my, are you so desperate for friends that now you're talking to a horse?"

Gabriel grinned in recognition of the voice and turned to see Andrea standing behind him. "Did you get settled?"

"Mostly. Settled but not unpacked. I thought I'd take a walk around. That's when I saw you here. Where's Liz?"

Gabriel straightened and nodded toward the barn. "In there. I'm giving her some breathing room for a while."

"You've already had an argument with her, haven't you?" Andrea tilted her head to one side and made a tsking sound. "I told Bill you were the wrong agent to send here. You don't know anything about getting along with women."

He glared at her. "Cut it out, Andrea."

She laughed and swatted at his arm. "I'm sorry, Gabriel. I couldn't help teasing you. Now let's get serious, and you catch me up on what's been going on since you've been here."

For the next several minutes he related everything he hadn't told her earlier in the kitchen—focusing on his suspicions about Bart Foster and Liz's feeling that he had lied to her by not telling him who he really was. When he'd finished, Andrea nodded.

"I'll give it a try and see if I can get close to her. But

it really doesn't matter whether she likes us or not as long as we keep our eyes and ears open and keep her safe."

Gabriel agreed. "I know. Maybe I need to go back in the barn and try to fix whatever went wrong with us."

"You do that," Andrea said. "I need to pick up some things in town. I'll go take care of that, and I'll see you at dinner."

Gabriel watched her go before he directed his gaze back to the barn. He had to find a way to make Liz feel more comfortable around him. He couldn't give up.

With that thought in mind, he strode toward the barn and into the alleyway.

When he stepped inside, he stopped and stared down the alleyway. Liz squatted beside a horse just outside the tack room as she rubbed liniment on his legs. He could hear the soft sound of her calming words as she stroked the horse.

The door at the other end of the alleyway was open. A shaft of sunlight dispersed its beams and circled her as if she sat in the middle of a spotlight. His gaze drifted over her as she concentrated on her task. He took in the pale curve of her neck, the thick eyelashes and the shock of golden hair that framed her gamine face. He stood as if rooted to the spot as he realized he'd never seen a woman to match her beauty, and he swallowed, trying to slow his pounding heart.

A slight movement caught his eye, and he peered past her to where Bart Foster stood just outside the open door at the other end of the barn. His gaze didn't waver as he stared at Liz. Gabriel stepped back a few inches in hopes Bart wouldn't see him, but he needn't have worried. Bart was too focused on watching Liz.

For a long moment, the boy just stared. Then his shoulders drooped, and he turned away and pulled out his cell phone. Gabriel moved into the barn and watched as Bart lifted his cell phone to his ear.

What was that all about? Who was Bart calling?

Gabriel glanced at Liz once more before he took a deep breath and walked toward her. He'd just witnessed something he didn't understand. Until he did, he intended to keep an eye on Bart Foster whether she liked it or not.

Liz looked up as he approached and then directed her attention back to the horse. He stopped beside her and stared down. Her fingers didn't slow in their work of wrapping the horse's leg.

"You look like you've done that before." She gnawed her lip and nodded as she continued her task. After a moment he sighed and squatted down beside her. "Liz, I think we need a do-over."

She finally gazed up, a confused look on her face. "What does that mean?"

Gabriel spied a bale of hay on the other side of the alley and pointed to it. "I'm going to sit down over there. When you're through with what you're doing, come sit with me and let's see if I can't make amends for upsetting you."

Her mouth opened, but she didn't speak. It was as if she was debating whether or not she wanted to listen to anything he had to say. Then she nodded and pushed to her feet. "All right. I'm through here. I'll put Cricket back in his stall, and then I'll be back."

He smiled as he stood. "I'll wait for you. I'll be the guy sitting on the hay bale."

Her mouth quirked as if she wanted to smile, but she ducked her head and led Cricket away. He walked over to the hay bale and sat down. Sweat popped out on his forehead, and he wiped at it.

Why was he so nervous all of a sudden? He'd faced vicious thugs and murderers, and he'd never felt any fear. But this was different. Earlier today they'd laughed and chatted as they mucked out the stalls and pushed the wheelbarrow to the compost pile. It had been a long time since he'd been so comfortable with anyone, especially a woman, and he wanted it back.

Liz walked over to where he sat and stopped in front of him. "Okay, here I am. What do you want to talk to me about?"

"I want…" he began, but the words froze in his mouth at the sight of a red laser dot focused on the center of Liz's forehead.

With a strangled cry, he lunged from the hay bale, tackled her around the legs and fell to the ground on top of her just as a bullet whizzed past their heads.

SEVEN

Liz heard the crack of the rifle as she fell to the floor. Her first thought was that she had to get out of there, but she couldn't move. Gabriel had her pinned to the ground. His body covered hers and his hands cradled her head. When there was no second shot, he rose in a crouch, grabbed her by the arm and dragged her into the stall next to the hay bale.

When they were inside, she started to straighten up, but he pushed her back down. "Stay here. Don't come out until I come back for you."

Panic seized her as he pulled out his gun and turned to leave. She reached out and clutched his arm. "Where are you going?"

"To see who's shooting at you."

She tightened her grip on his arm. "Don't leave me."

He patted her hand and smiled at her. "I'll be right back, Liz. I told you I would protect you, and that's what I intend to do. Now release me so I can see if the shooter's still outside."

At those words she grew even more frightened and

held on harder. What if he walked into a hail of gun-fire? He could be dead before he could get a shot off in return. "No, Gabriel. I'm afraid for you. I don't want you to die because of me."

A sad smile crossed his face, and he looked down at her hand on his arm. "It's been a long time since any-body's been concerned for my safety. It feels good, but I have to do this. I promise I'll be back in a few minutes."

Reluctantly she released him and nodded. "Be care-ful."

With one last glance at her, he eased out of the stall into the alley and flattened his body against the wall. He gripped his gun with both hands in front of him as he slid past the stalls toward the back door. After tak-ing a few steps, he disappeared from view. Liz lay on the ground, waiting for his return—her heart beating like a bass drum.

She didn't know how long she was alone in the stall, but it seemed like an hour before she heard Gabriel's voice. "I'm back, Liz. I couldn't find anyone. He must have gotten into the forest behind the barn and made his escape."

She wanted to stand, but her legs felt so weak she was afraid they would collapse. She sat up and brushed at her clothes. Her hands shook, which Gabriel must have noticed. He crouched down beside her and took her hands in his. "It's over now, Liz. You're safe."

Her lips trembled at the thought of how close she had come to death. "But what about the next time? What if you're not there to push me down? And worst of all, what if you're killed trying to protect me? I don't want to be the reason two people died."

He took hold of her shoulders, held her at arm's length and stared into her eyes. "You can't blame yourself for what happened to Kathy. You're not the reason she died. Daniel Shaw did that all by himself."

Tears welled in her eyes, and she blinked. "In my mind I know that, but my heart aches for her. She didn't deserve what happened to her."

He tightened his grip on her shoulders and pulled her a little closer. "And neither do you. We're going to get through this, and I'm going to get you back to Memphis to testify. I promise you that."

His eyes blazed with determination, and a feeling of relief surged through her. Despite the warmth and obvious sincerity of Dean and Gwen's welcome since she'd come here, she'd still felt so alone since Kathy's death. Now here was a man she'd known only a couple of days, and he was promising her he would protect her. Even after her accusations against him, he was willing to put his life on the line for her.

She swayed, and the next thing she knew, she had sagged against his chest. His hands slipped from her shoulders as his arms encircled her and held her tight against him. For a moment she stood there inhaling the scent of soap and the woodsy smell of his cologne. He pressed his cheek to the top of her head as his hand stroked her back.

"It's going to be all right, Liz."

Finally she pulled back and smiled up at him. "Thank you, Gabriel."

He raised his eyebrows. "For what?"

"For not giving up on me even after all my drama. I'm amazed you haven't asked to be relieved of baby-sitting a temperamental woman."

He chuckled and shook his head. "Temperamental? I think I'd describe you more as a woman with a fiery, quick temper."

"What?" She gasped and drew away from him, but he didn't let go of her.

His laugh echoed down the alleyway of the barn. "I'm teasing you, Liz. I really have a lot of respect for you. There aren't many people who would put their lives on the line because they wanted to do what's right. I'm going to do everything I can to help you."

Warmth rushed to her face, and she pulled out of his arms. "Then let's work together to make sure that Daniel Shaw gets everything that's coming to him."

She started to walk back to the door, but Gabriel caught her arm and turned her around. His eyes bore into hers, and he didn't speak right away. Then he swallowed. "There's one more thing I want you to know. I not only respect you, but I like you. There's something about you that's different from anyone else I've known in a long time. Even a job like mucking out the stalls becomes fun with you. I guess what I'm trying to say is that I'd really like to get to know you better. I think we could become good friends."

Liz hesitated before she answered. Gabriel seemed sincere, but so had her boyfriend when he borrowed all that money from her. Gabriel didn't appear to want anything from her, however, other than her friendship.

If she got to know him better, perhaps she could encourage him to face whatever had caused him so much pain in his life.

"I think we could, too," she said.

A relieved sigh escaped his mouth, and he smiled. "Great."

"Am I interrupting something?" The voice came from the doorway.

Liz glanced over her shoulder at Andrea, who walked down the alleyway toward them. She was struck once again at how beautiful Andrea was, but there was something aggressive, almost angry, in the way she strode toward them that caught Liz by surprise. She bit her lower lip and arched an eyebrow as she came closer.

Gabriel frowned when she stopped next to him. "Is something wrong, Andrea?"

She looked at Liz and then back to him. "Could I speak to you privately for a moment?"

"Sure."

"Excuse me. I need to get something from the tack room," Liz said as she turned away.

She moved quickly, but not fast enough to get out of earshot. She heard Andrea hiss at Gabriel, "You and Liz looked mighty friendly when I came in."

Liz slowed her steps in order to catch Gabriel's reply. "I was doing my job, Andrea. Nothing else."

"Well, see that it doesn't go any further. You know your judgment will be compromised if you get too involved with a victim."

"Cut it out," he said. "I know how to do my job."

The rest of their conversation was muffled once Liz

entered the tack room. A few minutes later she came out and walked back to where they still stood in quiet conversation. As she approached, she heard Gabriel ask, "Andrea, where have you been?"

"I told you I had to go to town to pick up a few things. I just got back. I thought I'd come check on you. Was everything quiet while I was gone?"

"We've had another attempt on Liz's life."

"Oh, no," Andrea gasped. She reached out and grabbed Liz's arm. "Are you all right? What happened?"

Gabriel quickly told her. When he was finished, he looked back at Liz. "We need to get you back to the house. Andrea and I will get on either side of you and make a run for it."

The muscles in Liz's throat constricted, and she cast a nervous look at the barn's open door. "Do you think the shooter might still be out there somewhere?"

Andrea patted her arm. "Don't worry, Liz. We'll take care of you. I'm sorry I wasn't here to help out earlier." She glanced at Gabriel. "I guess we'd both better stick close from now on."

He nodded. "I think you're right."

Gabriel and Andrea got on opposite sides of her. Gabriel's left arm circled her back and looped across Andrea's right one. They each held a gun. Together they paused at the entrance to the barn. Then, as if someone had given the starting command, the three of them dashed toward the house. She could see Gabriel's gaze sweeping the area as they ran. Andrea stared straight ahead as if her eyes were fixed on the finish line.

When they reached the back porch, Andrea released

her grip, grabbed her gun with both hands and whirled to guard them as Liz and Gabriel ran through the back door. Only then did she turn and follow them.

Gwen looked up from icing a cake at the kitchen counter and yanked her earbuds out when they burst through the door. She must have seen the terror on her face that Liz was feeling in her heart, because Gwen dropped the spoon she'd been stirring the frosting with and rushed to her. "What's the matter?"

"We've had another scare," Gabriel answered as Liz sank down in a chair at the table.

Gwen's face turned ashen. "What happened?"

"Somebody took a shot at Liz," Gabriel answered.

Gwen grabbed Liz by the arm and frowned. "A shot? I had my music on, and I didn't hear it. Are you okay?"

Liz nodded. "I'm fine, Gwen, thanks to Gabriel."

Andrea sat down facing her. "Liz, why don't you go up to your room while Gabriel and I tell Gwen what happened. I'll come up in a few minutes to check on you and bring you a cup of tea."

Liz started to protest, but she really didn't want to hear the shooting described. She needed to get away and be by herself for a while. She took a deep breath and pushed to her feet. "Thank you, Andrea. That sounds like a good idea."

She climbed the stairs to her room and once inside fell facedown on the bed. The memory of Gabriel pushing her to the ground returned, and she began to shake. Three attempts on her life. And all in the last two days.

She clutched her pillow and buried her face in it. The trial was still weeks away, and Shaw's men weren't going to give up. She doubted she'd survive another day at this rate. The desire to crawl beneath the covers of the bed and not come out until the trial overcame her, and she began to cry.

A sudden thought jolted her. She sat up, wiped her eyes and pulled open the drawer of the nightstand beside her bed. The Bible her mother gave her years ago lay inside, and she took it out. Almost as if her fingers knew where to go, she turned to the Scripture in Isaiah that her mother had read to her many times when she was having difficulties.

She read it again and smiled at the words.

Fear thou not; for I am with thee: be not dismayed; for I am thy God: I will strengthen thee; yea, I will help thee; yea, I will uphold thee with the right hand of my righteousness.

In that moment she knew what she had to do. She couldn't give in to fear. That's what Daniel Shaw expected her to do, but he was wrong. God controlled her life, not a drug dealer from Memphis.

Daniel Shaw had to face justice for what he did to Kathy, and with God's help she'd have the strength to get through the next weeks to make sure that he did.

Gabriel couldn't sleep. He'd tossed and turned for what he thought must be hours, but the clock showed it was only midnight. He couldn't get the three attempts on Liz's life off his mind. Somebody was determined to see that she didn't testify, and he knew who that somebody was. He'd never failed in an assignment yet, and he couldn't this time. It was becoming too important to him.

He rolled over and groaned at how scared he'd been when he looked up and saw the laser dot show up on her forehead. Instinct had kicked in, and he'd been able to knock her to the ground. The thing he worried about was whether or not he'd be able to do it the next time. Daniel Shaw wasn't about to give up, but neither was he.

Earlier when he had talked with Bill Diamond in the Memphis office, they'd discussed the possibility of moving Liz to a new location. The more he considered it, he thought it might a good decision. Bill seemed to think so, too.

After a few minutes, he threw back the covers and pulled on his jeans and T-shirt. Maybe he could find a snack in the kitchen. After he'd slipped on some shoes, he walked to the hallway and headed for the stairs. He paused outside Liz's room, but he heard no sound. Good. She was probably sleeping.

Quietly descending the stairs so as not to wake anyone, he made his way toward the kitchen. He was almost there when he noticed the light was on. Someone was in there. He eased up to the door and peered inside, but the room was empty.

"What are you doing up?"

He whirled at the sound of Liz's voice behind him. "I might ask you the same thing."

She shrugged. "Can't sleep. It's happened a lot lately."

"Yeah, I can understand that." He frowned. "Where were you?"

She held up a book. "Dean keeps a stack of books in the den for guests to use. I thought it might help me relax if I did some reading and drank a cup of hot chocolate. Would you like some?"

For the first time he noticed the pan on the kitchen stove. "Is that what's in that pot?"

She smiled and nodded. "My mother's special recipe for sleepless nights."

"I'd love to have some. I can't tell you how many cups I've drunk when I've been on assignment."

Her smile wavered a bit, and her eyes flickered. "Right. On assignments."

As she walked past him, he put his hand on her arm and stopped her. When she stared up at him, his heart raced. "Is that all you think you are?"

She didn't break eye contact with him. "That's what I am, Gabriel. An assignment that you are sworn to carry out. I don't kid myself into thinking anything else."

In that moment he wanted her to know that in the short time he'd known her, emotions that he'd thought long buried had begun to emerge. He didn't understand them yet, but he knew they were there. Not that he would act on them. It wasn't the time or place, and Liz, especially, couldn't afford for him to be distracted. But he had to make sure she knew how special she was. "Who's being cynical now?" he asked.

Her eyebrows shot up. "I'm not being cynical. I'm realistic. After this is all over and Daniel Shaw is in jail, we won't have any reason to see each other again. I know that, and so do you."

She was right in that that's how it had always been before, but something was different this time. "Do you remember what I said to you this afternoon before I sat down on that hay bale?"

"Yes. You said you thought we needed a do-over."

"We didn't get a chance to do that, but I still want to. What about you? Would you like to start over and get to know each other?"

She tilted her head to one side and smiled. "Yes. I'd like that very much."

He heaved a sigh of relief. "Then why don't we get ourselves some hot chocolate, sit down at the table and start again?"

She laughed, and he thought the sound was like tinkling bells. For the first time since he'd met her, she seemed truly relaxed, and he liked what he saw.

A few minutes later they were seated at the table facing each other. Gabriel took a sip from his cup, set it back in the saucer and crossed his arms on top of the table. "Now I want you to tell me all about yourself."

"Well…" she began, but he held up a hand to stop her.

"Wait. I don't want to know about Liz Madison, the woman who's hiding from a crazy drug dealer. I want to know the real Liz. Elizabeth Kennedy. What's she like? Where did she grow up? What are some of her favorite things to do?"

She looked at him as if she didn't know what to say, and then she stared down at her cup. "I grew up in a small town in Mississippi. I was an only child. After my parents died in a car crash when I was in college, I learned that I'd been adopted. I couldn't understand why they kept it from me. My faith got me through that time. Later I decided that maybe they were afraid I would try to find my birth parents, and they didn't want that to happen."

"Have you ever tried to find them?"

She shook her head. "No. They were my parents, and I didn't need any others." She exhaled a deep breath. "We lived on a farm, and my dad taught me to ride when I was a little girl. We'd ride together for hours across the fields, and he'd tell me about the crops he'd planted and what it was like growing up there when he was a little boy."

"Did your mom ride with you?"

"No. She liked to do other things. She read a lot and took me to the library in town at least once a week to get books. She made me a reader for life."

Gabriel smiled. "It sounds like you had a wonderful childhood."

"To my way of thinking, everything was perfect until my parents were killed. That's when I moved to Memphis and started working. I met a man and fell head over heels into what I thought was love with him. He asked me to marry him, and I was beyond thrilled. He had just started a business that was supposed to be our future, but he'd accumulated a lot of bills from what he called start-up costs. He asked if I could help him out, and I did to the tune of nearly everything my parents had left me. The money went to pay off his gambling debts, and I was left with no money and a fiancé who disappeared."

For a second Gabriel couldn't respond. Then he reached across the table and covered her hand with his. "That must have been rough."

"It was, but I survived just like I'd done before. I had forgotten how important God was to me when I'd come to Memphis, but after what happened with my fiancé I knew I couldn't face life without Him. I started going to the church where I met Kathy. She was the best friend I ever had, and she deserved to live a long and happy life."

Her mouth hardened into a thin line. The determination to find justice for her friend was etched into her face. He'd always wondered how people survived when bad things happened to them. Now he knew. It was something he'd never understood—faith.

"What about you?" she asked.

He jerked his attention back to her. "I grew up on a ranch in Texas. My mother died when I was young, and my father raised me. He was great. He never missed one of my football games when I was in school. We even tried our hand at some rodeo events for a while. He rode broncs, and I rode bulls."

Liz giggled. "You on the back of a bucking bull? It's hard for me to imagine that."

He grinned. "I'll have you know I was a good rider, even won a little money. I made the college team and participated in events until I graduated. Then I went back home after college to help my dad run the ranch, but he died soon after."

Sadness flickered in Liz's eyes. "I'm sorry. That must have been hard."

"It was, but I managed for a while. Then I became engaged to my high school sweetheart, and we were to be married. The day of the wedding the best man, my friend since childhood, brought me a letter from her. She said she couldn't marry me because she didn't love me. She left town, and I didn't see her for a few months."

"So she came back. What happened then?"

"She married my friend, the best man who'd brought me the letter. Apparently they'd been in love for a while, but they hadn't acted on it because of respect for me. I ended my friendships with both of them, sold the farm and applied to the FBI. I've been married to my job ever since."

"Do you know where they are now?"

He sighed and rubbed his neck. "Yeah, they're married and have two kids." He tried to keep his voice neutral, but he could feel the way bitterness twisted his expression. He wanted to say he'd moved on from the experience, but he knew he hadn't.

She stared at him for a moment before she leaned toward him. "Let me ask you something. Has hanging on to your resentment and blaming them for not getting what you wanted in life made you happy?"

He sat back in his chair and thought about what she'd just asked. "No. What are you getting at, Liz?"

"It's simple, really. You've stewed over what happened. Meanwhile, your friends are living their lives, probably happy as can be, and you're caught up in anger, resentment and blame. You've let those feelings rob you of the joy that God wants to bring into your life."

A sarcastic laugh rumbled in his throat. "You make it sound so easy."

She shook her head. "I never said it was easy, because first you have to give up your own will to hold on to those feelings. It's tempting to hold on to grudges, but it's only when you let God take them away that He can replace them with all the good things He has waiting for you in life." She squeezed his hand. "I've only known you a short time, Gabriel, but I can tell you're a good man. You're cheating yourself out of what God has planned for you."

She pushed the book that she'd brought into the kitchen across the table, and he stared down at it. "What's this?"

"It's a Bible," she said. "I find a lot of comfort in its pages. You could, too, if you'd allow yourself." She thumbed through the pages and then pointed to a passage. "This is one of my favorite passages."

He looked down, and the words seemed to leap off the page.

Trust in the LORD with all thine heart; and lean not unto thine own understanding. In all thy ways acknowledge him, and he shall direct thy paths.

He took in the passage, then glanced up at her. "I don't know if I can do that or not."

She smiled. "I'll be praying that you do." She eyed

the clock on the wall and rose from the table. "I need to get to bed. Morning comes awfully early around here."

She picked up her cup, but he waved his hand to stop her. "Don't bother with the dishes. I'm not sleepy. I'll take care of them."

His heart thudded when she looked at him. "Thanks. I enjoyed our do-over, Gabriel. I'll see you in the morning."

She was almost to the door when he called out to her. "Liz, wait."

She turned. "What?"

He licked his lips. He had something to say, and he wanted it to come out right. "I enjoyed this time with you, too. I just want you to know that whether you call yourself Liz Madison or Elizabeth Kennedy, it really doesn't matter. Both are the same woman, and I think she's pretty special."

She didn't say anything, but the way her face lit up, he knew she was pleased. He watched as she left the room. After she was gone, he looked back down at the Scripture she'd pointed out to him and read it again.

He didn't understand yet how he could do what the words said, but it seemed to be working for Liz. And he wanted the peace she had in her life. According to her, all he had to do was reach out and accept it. He wished he could, but the old feelings surged to the forefront to remind him of what people he'd loved and trusted had done to him.

After a moment he closed the book and stared at the door with the hope that Liz would come back. But she didn't. All he could do was look forward to tomorrow and the time that he would spend with her. He suddenly realized that this was the first time since the day he'd been jilted that he'd wanted to spend time with a woman.

He'd been truthful with Liz. She was a special person.

EIGHT

There had been no new attempts on her life in the last week, and Liz was beginning to feel less apprehensive than she'd been. Although Dean had insisted she didn't have to work while she was here, she found it took her mind off her problems for a while. She'd come to look forward to spending the mornings at the barn with Gabriel helping her muck the stalls and take care of the horses. She'd suggested several times that they go riding, but he'd vetoed the idea every time. Just because there hadn't been any new attacks didn't mean that the danger was gone. They had to stay alert at all times.

Her afternoons had been spent with Andrea, and she had come to like her very much. Gwen had been wonderful about offering companionship since she'd been at Little Pigeon, but she didn't have a lot of free time.

School had started a few weeks earlier, and Gwen was involved with her daughter, Maggie, and all the school activities that seemed to hit in the early fall, in addition to all the work at the ranch. Then there was an influx of guests who came for the brilliant colors of the trees in the Smokies at this time of year. Having Andrea to talk to had made the days slip by faster, and they couldn't go fast enough. She wanted the trial to be over and her life to go back to normal.

A loud sneeze pulled her from her thoughts, and she glanced over her shoulder at Andrea, who sat on a hay bale across from where she was cleaning out the hoof of a horse that had just come back from a trail ride.

"Bless you," Liz automatically responded as Andrea sneezed again.

Andrea pulled a tissue from her pocket and wiped at her nose. "In case you didn't know, I'm allergic to hay."

Liz released the horse's leg and stared at her. "I'm sorry. I wouldn't have brought you down here this afternoon if I'd known. Maybe Gabriel can come and relieve you."

Andrea shook her head. "No, he deserves some downtime to relax and not have to be on guard after he spent the morning with you. Not that it could have been that hard on him, since he seemed to have a grand time, although I can't imagine why anybody would want to clean out stalls." She swept her arm in a wide circle to encompass all the barn. "I don't understand how anybody gets enjoyment out of working with those animals. Horses scare me just to look at them."

Liz smiled. "Did you have a bad experience with a horse when you were little?"

Andrea shrugged. "Not that I know of. They're just so…so big."

Liz laughed at that. "Yeah, they're big, all right."

At that moment Andrea's cell phone chimed with

an incoming text, and she pulled it from her pocket. She read the words on the screen and then stared up at the ceiling and huffed out a big breath of air. "I don't believe it!"

"What?"

Andrea pointed to the text. "It's a guy I've been dating. He's a nice guy, but the more I get to know him I realize how different we are. I've tried to break it off with him, but he won't take no for an answer. Well, maybe he'll understand when I give him my final no." She began to tap out a text but suddenly stopped. "Oh, no."

Andrea stared at her phone, an angry expression on her face.

"What's the matter?"

"Suddenly, I have no bars. What's with the cell service around here?"

Liz laughed. "It happens all the time. It's because we're in the mountains, I think."

Andrea gritted her teeth, then released a sigh. "It's just as well. I probably would have said something I'd regret later."

Liz reached for the hoof pick and raised the horse's leg again. "So you've been dating someone? I had the impression that maybe you and Gabriel…" She let her voice trail off.

"That'll be the day, when I fall for a player like Gabriel Decker. You need to be careful, Liz. I wouldn't want you to get hurt."

Liz's face burned, and she focused on her task. "Gabriel and I are just friends, like you and I are."

"That's what you say now, but I know how charming

he can be when he wants to be. Don't think it'll ever go any farther with Gabriel. He's dated a lot of women since I've known him, but he never goes out with any of them over two or three times. He's got his eye on becoming a special agent in charge at one of the FBI offices. He doesn't know I overheard him talking to Bill Diamond about an opening that's coming up soon in Texas. It seems like he wants to go back home."

Liz's heart plunged to the pit of her stomach. Of course Gabriel wanted to advance in his career, and if that was important to the man, then she wanted it for him. Andrea had also told her what she'd suspected. He'd had lots of women in his life.

He'd told her she was special the night they'd spent time in the kitchen, but that was probably a line he used on all his conquests. She raised her eyebrows at the thought. Conquests? Was that what she was?

She shook her head. The last thing she needed was to fall for Gabriel Decker. He'd told her himself that he was married to his job, and now Andrea had told her that he was looking at a position a thousand miles away from the Smokies.

She took a deep breath and gritted her teeth. She was losing focus on what was important—testifying at Daniel Shaw's trial. She couldn't allow anything to distract her from doing what she'd set out to do. Falling for Gabriel Decker was one of the last things she needed to happen right now.

With a sigh, she released the horse's leg and stroked her mane. "Good girl. Now let's give you a rubdown, and I'll let you rest in your stall."

The wooden box that she kept all her grooming supplies in sat at her feet. She reached down to get the container of liniment she always kept in there, but it was gone. Probably one of the other employees had taken it to use on another horse.

"What's the matter?" Andrea asked.

"My liniment is gone. It's always right here, but it isn't today."

Andrea pushed up from the hay bale. "I'll go get you another container. Where do you keep it? In the tack room?"

Liz shook her head. "No. I'll have to go to the workshop and get some more. Do you think you can hold this horse's reins until I get back?"

Andrea's eyes went round, and she gulped. "You know I'm afraid of horses."

Liz laughed. "Don't be scared. I'll be back before you know it. Just stand here and talk to her if she gets restless."

Andrea pursed her lips and arched an eyebrow. "If she gets restless, I'm letting go of the reins and running for my life before she tramples me."

Liz thrust the reins into Andrea's hands. "You are so funny. Just keep saying to yourself, 'I can do this. I can do this.'"

Before Andrea could refuse, Liz hurried to the door. She smiled as she heard Andrea repeating over and over, "I can do this. I can do this."

As she ran from the barn to the workshop, she remembered that Dean had told her a few days ago that he had put a new combination padlock on the door. He'd told her the sequence of numbers, and she'd repeated it at the time. Now she wasn't so sure she could remember it correctly. Her forehead puckered as she tried to recall what he'd said.

When she arrived at the door, she took a breath and entered the numbers as she remembered. To her relief, the lock popped open. She looped the shackle over the backplate that was attached to the door and left it hanging open.

Once inside, she headed quickly toward the doorway into the adjacent room and to the cabinets where all the medicines were kept. Maybe what she needed would be on one of the lower shelves and she'd be able to reach it. Bart wasn't around to help her today.

She opened the first cabinet and scanned the interior. No liniment there. It took several minutes to search all the other cabinets. When she finished, she propped her hands on her hips and frowned. Where could all the liniment have gone? She was certain they had several containers of it just a few days ago.

Maybe Dean could tell her. She reached for her cell phone and then remembered. She had left it on the wooden chest in the barn. She'd have to go ask Dean in person if they were out of liniment.

She stretched up to close the last cabinet door and froze at the sound of the door clicking shut. Strange. There wasn't enough wind today to blow the door closed. She retraced her steps to the door. When she stopped at it, she turned the knob and pushed, but the door didn't budge.

Thinking it was stuck, she gave it a harder shove,

but it still wouldn't move. Fear raced up her spine like an electric jolt as she realized the door wasn't going to open. Someone had closed the padlock, and she was now a prisoner in the workshop.

There was no need to worry, though. It was probably just an accident—someone seeing the door open and assuming that it needed to be shut and locked back up again. Andrea knew where she'd gone. If she wasn't back in a few minutes, she'd come looking for her. She just had to be patient until Andrea got here. A chair sat at the side of the room, and she headed toward it but stopped and gagged at the horrible smell that assaulted her. She wasn't sure what rotten eggs smelled like, but that's what the odor made her think of.

She jerked her head around and stared at the portable propane heater that Dean used in the winter. Her heart leaped into her throat when she saw that the line running from the two propane tanks that sat behind the heater was disconnected, and gas fumes were pouring into the room.

She rushed across the floor and knelt down as she tried frantically to figure out how to reconnect the line and stop the escaping gas, but it was no use. Dizziness overtook her, and she felt as if she'd throw up any minute.

Desperate to find a way out, she pushed to her feet and scanned the room for something, anything, that would help her escape. The chair. She could break a window out with the chair.

She stumbled over and picked up the chair, even though her vision was beginning to weaken. The chair felt as if it weighed a hundred pounds, but she picked it up and staggered to the window. Panting, she wrapped her hands around the back of the chair and with sheer willpower drew back and tried to swing it at the window. It was no use, though. Her strength had deserted her.

The chair tumbled from her grasp, and she dropped to the floor. Her last thought before she closed her eyes was that Daniel Shaw had finally won.

Gabriel couldn't sit still. For some the fact that no more threats or attacks against Liz had surfaced in the last week would be welcome news. For him it only made him wonder what Shaw's gang was planning next. For the fourth time he paced across the floor of his room and stopped at the window. He couldn't explain the restless feeling that he had. He'd always had an instinct for trouble, and he had the feeling that something bad was about to happen. He didn't know what, but he couldn't shake the sense that it wasn't far off.

He pulled his hand through his hair and groaned. He shouldn't have taken the afternoon off, even though Andrea was with Liz. The thought had no sooner popped into his head than he dismissed it. Andrea was a good agent. She'd proven herself many times in the field. It was time for him to relax and think about something else.

As he stood at the window, he pulled the curtain back and gazed out at the barn. Suddenly he saw Liz hurry out of the stable and run toward the workshop. She opened the door and disappeared inside.

At that moment a knock sounded at his bedroom door, and a voice called out, "Housekeeping."

Gabriel opened his door for the young woman who'd cleaned his room ever since he'd been at Little Pigeon. She smiled. "I'm getting ready to go home, Mr. Decker, and I wanted to check and see if you need anything before I leave."

He smiled back at her. "No, thank you, Mandy. You have a good night."

"You, too," she said as he closed the door.

He stood there for a second thinking about this dark mood that seemed to be hovering over him. He ambled back to the window, pulled the curtain back and stared at the workshop. The door was closed and locked now. Liz must have gone back to the barn.

Letting out a bored sigh, he moved back to the bed and sat down on it. Maybe a nap would help pass the time, since he couldn't seem to concentrate on anything. Yet for some reason, he couldn't lie down. He was too antsy. Maybe he'd just walk down to the barn and see what Liz and Andrea were up to this afternoon.

A few minutes later as he approached the barn, he could hear Andrea's voice. She kept saying the same words over and over. "That's a good girl. That's a good girl. That's a good girl."

He stopped at the entrance to the barn and laughed at the sight of Andrea standing in the alleyway and holding the reins of a horse. "What are you doing?" he asked.

She cast an angry glare over her shoulder. "What does it look like? I'm holding a horse."

"I thought you didn't like horses."

"I don't," she snarled. "I'm holding on to this one until Liz gets back."

Her last words caught his attention. "Gets back from where?"

"The workshop. She went to get some liniment. I don't know what's taking her so long."

Chills radiated down his spine. "And you didn't go look for her?"

Andrea's face paled, and she swallowed. "Oh, Gabriel, you don't think…"

He didn't give her time to complete her sentence. He jerked the reins from her hands, looped them over the top board of a stall and ran toward the door. "Come on!"

Gabriel's heart was in his throat as they raced across the ground toward the workshop. If something had happened to Liz, he would never forgive himself. When he skidded to a stop at the door, he saw that the padlock was closed. His first thought was that she had locked the door herself after exiting and gone up to the house for something. Then he thought better of it. She wouldn't do that. She wouldn't want to keep Andrea waiting with the horse.

He raised his fist and pounded on the door. "Liz! Liz! Are you in there?"

There was no answer.

"Maybe she went up to the house," Andrea said. "I'll go look for her there."

She took off running before he could answer her. He swiveled and scanned the area around the workshop, but Liz was nowhere to be seen. Frantic, he moved to the window, shaded his face with his hands and peered into the dark interior of the room. He was about to turn away when something caught his attention. An overturned chair lay a few feet past the window, and he could see a booted foot underneath. He recognized Liz's boots right away.

His heart almost exploded at the sight, and he rushed back to the padlocked door. He drew back and kicked the door with all his might, but the lock held tight. The second kick didn't work either. Then he pulled his gun from the holster, stood back and shot the backplate that held the lock.

Wood around it splintered at the impact, and the screws holding it in place sagged downward but didn't give up their hold. He reared back once more and with a loud cry kicked at the door with everything he had. The door gave way as the hinges pulled loose. One shove, and he was in the workshop.

The smell of gas assaulted him the minute he entered the room, and he glanced over at the propane heater. What had happened to make it malfunction? He didn't know, but there was no time to worry about that now. He had to get Liz out of here. Holding his breath, he picked her up, cradled her in his arms and rushed outside with her.

He got her several dozen feet away from the building before he laid her on the ground and gave her a gentle shake. "Liz! Can you hear me?"

A low moan was his only answer.

"What happened?" he heard Andrea cry out.

He looked up to see her dashing toward them. "Liz

was inside and there was a gas leak. She needs to get to the hospital right away." He pulled his cell phone from his pocket and groaned. "I don't have any cell service. There's a landline in the tack room. Go in there and call 911. Tell them to get here as quickly as they can."

Andrea didn't hesitate but took off running for the barn. Gabriel tilted Liz's head back. He leaned forward as he tried to detect any sign of breathing. There was none. She needed artificial respiration now. Fortunately, he was trained in CPR.

He pinched her nostrils closed and placed his mouth over hers, making a complete seal. Then he exhaled directly into her mouth, released her nostrils and mouth, and sat back to check for chest rise. He was about to decide she wasn't going to respond when a sudden burst of air filled her chest, and she exhaled.

For a moment all he could do was stare at her chest rising and falling, and then he covered his eyes with his hands and shook his head in relief. She wasn't out of the woods yet, but she wasn't dead.

Andrea ran out of the barn and back to where he sat. "They'll be here right away. How is she?"

"She's alive." His voice cracked on the last word.

What if he hadn't come to the barn in time? She might be dead right now. He couldn't think like that. He *had* come to the barn, and Liz was breathing.

In the distance he heard the sound of a siren, and he bent and whispered in her ear. "Help is on the way. Hang in there. I don't want to lose you now."

NINE

There had been no updates on Liz since she was rushed into the emergency room. Gabriel had stood helplessly as the EMTs wheeled the gurney through the sliding doors at the ambulance bay. Unable to enter there, he'd made his way to the waiting room, where he now sat with Gwen and Andrea.

He stood and strode over to the receptionist's desk. She must have seen him coming, because she suddenly became focused on her computer screen and didn't look up when he stopped in front of her. He waited a moment for her to acknowledge him. When she didn't, he tapped on the window.

"Miss, may I have your attention?"

She looked up with exasperation on her face. "What is it now, Mr. Decker?"

"I need to know how Miss Madison is. We haven't heard anything."

The woman sighed and shook her head. "You've told me that the last five times you've been to my desk, and my answer is still the same. The doctor will let you know when he can. Now, why don't you sit down and be patient? It won't be much longer."

He wasn't about to get any information out of her, and he frowned as he stormed back to his seat. "What did she say?" Andrea asked.

He slumped in his chair and rubbed his hands over his eyes. "The same thing she said before. The doctor will let us know something soon."

From the chair next to him Gwen reached over and patted his arm. "Don't worry, Gabriel. She's going to be fine."

"I hope so."

He gritted his teeth and leaned back in his chair with his eyes closed and recalled watching Liz enter the workshop. If he hadn't gone to answer the knocking at his door at that moment, he would have seen who locked the door behind her, but he hadn't. Now all he could do was berate himself for not being with her. From now on both he and Andrea would be at her side at all times.

"Coffee, anyone?" He opened his eyes and saw Dean striding into the room, carrying a container with four cups of coffee. "I went to the cafeteria and got this for us."

Gwen and Andrea took their cups and settled back in their chairs. Gabriel pushed to his feet. "No, thanks. I think I'll check with the receptionist again."

Dean caught him by the arm before he'd gotten halfway across the room. "Gabriel, calm down. We have to let the doctors and nurses do what they're trained to do."

He turned and glared at Dean. "And we're supposed to sit here and do nothing?"

Dean set the container that still held two cups down on a table and inhaled deeply. "Come with me."

Without waiting for a reply he headed to the other side of the waiting room. Gabriel started to protest but decided it would do no good. He followed Dean and dropped down in one of the chairs. Dean took the other one and scooted closer. Then he leaned forward and clasped his hands in front of him.

"Gabriel, we have something very important to do while we're waiting. We need to pray for Liz."

"Pray?" Andrea and Gwen as well as the receptionist behind her glass panel jerked their heads up and stared at him. His skin warmed, and he lowered his voice. "What good is that going to do?"

"It's going to do a lot of good. We need to ask God to watch over her, and we need to ask that the doctors know what to do to save her life. We also need to pray for peace that we can accept God's will."

Dean's words shocked him. "His will?" he snapped. "Was it God's will for this to happen in the first place? What has Liz ever done that she deserves something like this to happen to her? All she wants is to put a murderer behind bars, and she's suffering for it."

"Gabriel, you know as well as I do that Liz placed her life in God's hands. That's how she's been able to face everything that's happened. He's been by her side, taking care of her all along."

Gabriel's pulse raced as he remembered seeing her go into that workshop. "Well, He's not doing a very good job of it. Where was He this afternoon when someone was locking her in a building filled with propane gas?"

"He was watching over her, protecting her."

Gabriel leaned toward Dean and clenched his teeth. "How can you say that? She was almost killed," he hissed.

A slow smile spread across Dean's face, and he shook his head. "You're missing the point." He paused for a moment and studied Gabriel's face. "Let me ask you something. I saw you right after Liz and Andrea went to the barn. You said you hadn't slept well the night before and thought you'd take a nap. Why didn't you?"

The question surprised Gabriel. "I don't know. I felt restless. I couldn't be still."

"And then?"

"I looked out the window and saw Liz going in the workshop. The next time I looked, the door was closed and locked. I thought she'd gone back to the barn."

"So why didn't you lie down then and take your nap?"

Gabriel shrugged. "I don't know. Something kept bothering me, like I needed to go check on her and Andrea. I decided I wasn't going to have any peace until I did. That's when I found out she'd never come back from the workshop."

"And because you went to the barn, Liz's life was saved. Just think what would have happened if you'd lain down on the bed and gone to sleep."

Gabriel's breath hitched in his throat. "She'd be dead right now."

Dean's face lit up with a smile. "Exactly. She's still alive because God was watching over her. He was there with her this afternoon, but He was also there with you."

Gabriel didn't say anything as he thought about what Dean had said. Then he swallowed and stared back at Dean. "Do you really think God led me to go to the workshop?"

Dean nodded. "I do. How else can you explain that nagging feeling that something wasn't right? You weren't just an FBI agent this afternoon. You were an agent on assignment from a much higher power."

Liz had told him about her faith, and now Dean had shown him his. Could they be right? Had he been missing something all these years that could have brought him peace?

Before he could ask Dean anything else, the doors to the treatment rooms opened, and a young man who looked like he could barely be out of college emerged. A stethoscope hung around his neck. "Who's here with Miss Madison?"

"We are," Gabriel responded as all four of them jumped to their feet and hurried toward the man.

When they reached him, the man looked from one to another and smiled. "I'm Dr. Jacobson. I have been treating Miss Madison, and she appears to be recovering nicely. She's going to have a bad headache, but other than that, everything else looks good. Vital signs are right on target. She's got some pretty terrific timing. If she'd been discovered a few minutes later, we'd be having a different conversation right now."

Gabriel opened his mouth to speak, but his vocal cords felt frozen. He relaxed when Dean spoke up. "When will she be able to go home?"

"We're going to keep her overnight for observation,

just to make sure everything is okay. She'll probably be released in the morning."

"Thank you, Dr. Jacobson," Dean said as he shook the man's hand.

Gabriel stuck out his hand, but he still couldn't speak. After shaking the doctor's hand, he turned and walked back to the chair where he'd been sitting. He dropped down in it, propped his elbows on his knees and buried his face in his hands.

Across the room he could hear Dean still asking questions about Liz. All he needed to know right now was that she was all right. *Thank You, God, for taking care of her.*

His muscles tensed, and he sat up, his mouth gaping open. He couldn't believe what had just happened. He had prayed for the first time in his life. He didn't know if it meant anything or not, but he couldn't ignore the peaceful feeling that washed over him.

In the past whenever he hadn't understood something, he would ponder it until it made sense to him. Sometimes that would take days, other times not so long. He had no idea if he'd ever be able to wrap his mind around all the things Liz and Dean had said to him about God.

He just couldn't see how this thing they called faith could be something he'd ever be able to understand.

Liz heard the voices before she opened her eyes. She lay still as the sound buzzed around her. She wished she could make sense of what they were saying, but her head was hurting so badly she couldn't concentrate. After a few minutes she forced her eyes open and stared up.

An unfamiliar white ceiling appeared overhead, and she wondered where she could be. She turned her head on the pillow and stared at Gabriel in a chair beside her bed. A voice from the other side said something, and she looked to see Andrea sitting there. She raised her hand and rubbed her eyes.

Gabriel must have seen the movement, because he was out of his chair in an instant and was bent over her. "Liz," he said, "are you awake?"

She tried to speak, but her mouth was so dry she couldn't make the words come out. All she could think about was how thirsty she was and how she wished she had a cool drink of water. Gabriel must have read her mind; the next thing she knew, he was hovering over her with a cup and a straw angled toward her mouth.

She clamped her lips around the straw and almost sighed with pleasure at the cool drink that poured into her mouth. She took a deep breath and started to draw another sip, but Gabriel pulled the cup away. "Don't take too much too fast. We don't want it to make you sick."

Someone touched her arm opposite Gabriel, and when she turned her head, Andrea was standing there, a worried expression on her face. "Oh, Liz. I'm so glad you're awake."

She frowned and looked from Gabriel to Andrea. What had happened? She searched her mind for a hint of why she was lying in this bed, and then it came back to her. The workshop, the propane gas and the locked door.

Her eyes widened, and the panic that had filled her when she realized the door was padlocked from the outside washed over her again. She gasped and tried to sit up in bed, but Gabriel put his hands on her shoulders and pushed her back down. "It's all right, Liz. You're safe now. We're here with you."

"How…how did you…?" She couldn't get her thoughts to come out, and she stopped in frustration.

Gabriel put his hand on her forehead and brushed her hair back out of her eyes. "Shhh," he whispered. "Don't try to talk. We'll explain everything when you're feeling better. For now just rest and heal. Andrea and I will be right here. We won't leave you alone."

His hand had drifted down so that it now lay against her cheek, and it gave Liz a comforting feeling. For the first time in years she felt as if she wasn't alone. Gabriel was here, and he'd make sure she was okay while she slept.

With a contented sigh, she reached up and stroked his hand, then closed her eyes. She didn't move as his hand continued to caress her cheek. It felt so right, as if he had the power to banish all the bad things from her life and make everything right. She had never felt such a strong connection from another person's touch.

In that instant just before sleep overtook her, she discovered something that she should have seen days ago. She was starting to care for Gabriel Decker. It was foolish of her. He was going away, maybe to Texas, and she might never see him again, but that didn't matter right now. Her heart was opening up for him, whether she wanted it to or not.

* * *

Gabriel wanted to wrap his arms around Liz and keep her close forever, but Andrea was in the room. She might think such a display was unprofessional, and he didn't want to give her any reason to judge him that way.

So he silently stood there, bent over the bed, and watched Liz sleep with her cheek resting against his palm. After a few minutes he pulled his hand away, sat down in the chair and scooted closer to Liz.

He stared at her as if he needed to memorize every detail of her face. As he did, he reaffirmed what he'd known since the first time he saw her. She was the most beautiful woman he'd ever seen. Since then his opinion hadn't changed. It had only become stronger.

She lay so still in sleep with her hair fanned out around her head on the pillow. She looked like a princess lying there, and he'd never wanted anything in his life like he wanted to protect her from any harm or sadness or pain. He wanted her to know how he thought she was the best and bravest person he'd ever known and that he couldn't imagine anything better than staying by her side.

But he couldn't.

She might be a princess, but the truth of the matter was that he was no Prince Charming. She had been right when she told him that his anger had turned his soul dark. He'd carried around so much baggage for years that he didn't know if he could ever make a woman happy, especially one like Liz.

"I think I'll go get some coffee. You want some?"

Andrea's voice interrupted his thoughts. "It's going to be a long night."

He nodded without looking up at her. "Sounds good. Make mine black."

"I know how you take your coffee, Gabriel. This isn't our first assignment together."

Surprised at her words, he glanced up. His heart dropped into his stomach at the grim line of Andrea's mouth. Her words hinted that she knew Liz was becoming more than an assignment to him.

"Andrea…" he began.

She held up her hand to stop him. "All I'm saying is that you can't allow yourself to become distracted. If you do, you're putting all our lives in danger."

Before he could answer, she swept past him and out the door. He sat there for a moment staring after her. Then he shook his head. He reached for Liz's hand, raised it to his lips and kissed it.

"What am I going to do, Liz?" he whispered. "I told you once that you're special, and you are. There's no one like you in the world. But you deserve someone better than me, someone who shares your beliefs and can face life with you filled with hope. That's not me. So when this is over, I'm going to get as far away from you as I can. Maybe then you can find the life you deserve."

The words were barely out of his mouth when a knock at the door startled him. "Come in."

The door opened, and Dean and Sheriff Whitman entered the room. He stood to greet the men. "Dean, I thought you'd taken Gwen home."

"I did, but Ben came by to talk to you, and I came back with him."

Gabriel's senses automatically went on high alert at Ben's somber expression. If he'd made a special trip to the ranch to see him, there had to be a reason. "What's up, Ben?"

Ben glanced at Liz and tilted his head toward the hall. "Why don't we step outside so we don't disturb Liz?"

Gabriel didn't want to leave her alone, but from Ben's tone of voice and body language, he knew something was wrong. "Okay."

They stepped into the hall and Gabriel closed the door behind him. Ben exhaled a breath and looked around to see if anyone was within earshot. "A couple was driving through Cades Cove this morning and spotted what they thought was a body in the trees just beyond the road. They called us, and we retrieved the body. It was Gene Curtis."

Gabriel's mouth fell open. "The guy who attacked Liz in the parking lot?"

Ben nodded. "Yeah. He'd been shot and his body dumped there."

Gabriel put his hands to his eyes and scrubbed down his face. "I know this answer, but I have to ask anyway. Do you have any leads?"

Ben shook his head. "Not a one. The body has been sent to Nashville for an autopsy. Maybe something will show up that points us to a suspect, but I doubt it. It looks like a mob hit to me."

Gabriel jerked his head around and stared at the door

to Liz's room. "So assuming Curtis was sent here as a hit man, he was taken out because he failed his assignment."

"That's what I'm thinking," Ben said.

"Which means," Dean added, "Curtis couldn't have locked Liz in the workshop, because he was already dead."

Gabriel ran his hand through his hair and groaned. "Yeah, and it also means there is another killer that we don't know about yet. Someone able to take down Curtis, who definitely knew how to defend himself. So where do we go from here?"

Ben pulled off the Stetson that he always wore and held it in front of him. "I think I have an idea."

Gabriel gave his attention to the sheriff. "What is it, Ben?"

"I called Bill Diamond in Memphis. I think we need to send Liz somewhere else until the trial."

Gabriel's heart pounded. "Send her somewhere else? Does that mean I'm being taken off the case?"

Ben shook his head. "Not at all. It just means we have to find a safer place, one where whoever's trying to kill her won't find her."

"And where would that be?"

Ben hooked his fingers in his uniform's waistband and let his hat continue to dangle on his other fingers. "I think Mount LeConte would be a good place."

Gabriel frowned. "I've heard of the place, but I don't know much about it."

Ben pursed his lips for a moment. "Yeah. It's a popular place in the Smokies. It's not the highest mountain.

In fact, it's the third highest, at a little over sixty-three hundred feet. The only way to get there is to hike up one of the five trails leading to the top. The shortest one is about five miles, but it's a strenuous climb. Once you get to the top, there are some rustic lodges that hikers can rent. There's a dining room, and meals are served. No TV, electricity or any of the other comforts of modern living in the cabins, but the scenery is worth it all. It's isolated, not the kind of place someone could really sneak in or out of without being noticed, so it should be easier for you to keep anyone dangerous at bay."

"Can you get a cabin there right now?" Dean interrupted. "I know there are a lot of tourists in the mountains to see the fall foliage. Wouldn't everything already be booked up?"

Ben nodded. "I talked with the office who takes care of reservations. They had a cancellation, and they decided that police business made it to the top of the waiting list. So you're all set. You can leave day after tomorrow—giving Liz time to recover from this ordeal before she has to do any hiking—and follow the llamas up the mountain."

Gabriel's eyebrows arched. "Did you say llamas?"

"Yeah. It's the only way supplies are carried up to the lodge. On the backs of llamas. They used mules for a while, but their hooves did so much damage to the trail they decided to try llamas. It works fine. They go up three times a week."

Gabriel thought for a moment before he spoke. "Do you think we can keep her safe there?"

"I do. Only you, Andrea, Gwen and Dean will know

where she is except me. I think we can keep her under-cover up there until it's time to head back to Memphis for the trial."

Gabriel turned to Dean. "What do you think, Dean? You and Ben know this area a lot better than I do. Do you think this will work?"

Dean nodded. "I think we have to get her somewhere and keep her hidden for the next few weeks. What better place than on a high mountain in the middle of the Smokies?"

A remote mountaintop, away from the rest of the world, with lots of time to think about the things that were troubling him. Not only could it be a safe place for Liz, it could provide him with the perfect environ-ment to come to grips with the questions Dean and Liz had stirred in his heart.

Just then the elevator down the hall opened, and An-drea walked out holding two cups of coffee. She smiled when she saw Ben and Dean. "Hi, guys," she said. "Did you come to check on Liz?"

"Yeah," Ben said, "but we really came to talk to you and Gabriel about getting Liz to a safe place once she's ready to leave the hospital."

She handed Gabriel one of the cups and wrapped her fingers around the other one. "Do you have a place in mind?"

Ben nodded. "It's the best I can come up with at the moment."

She turned back to Gabriel. "Well, don't keep me in suspense. Where are we taking her?"

Gabriel glanced from Dean and Ben to Andrea, then

took a deep breath. "Let me put it this way, Andrea. If you don't have a good pair of hiking shoes, you'd better get some, because you're about to take a really long walk with a pack train of llamas."

TEN

Two mornings later Liz stood at the Trillium Gap trail-head with Gabriel and Andrea as they waited to begin their hike to the summit of Mount LeConte. At first Liz hadn't been too enthusiastic about the trip, but Gabriel and Dean had convinced her it would be the best place for her right now. From what they'd said, an assassin would have to be very determined if he made the steep climb up the mountain—and it would be difficult for him to arrive at the campsite without anyone noticing.

As they waited, she let her gaze drift over Gabriel and Andrea as they stood to the side of the trail in a deep discussion. Ever since she'd been dismissed from the hospital, Gabriel had been withdrawn and aloof with her, not at all like he was before the attack. She had the feeling that something was bothering him but that he didn't want her to know what it was. She had wanted to ask him why he seemed to be avoiding her, but she hadn't been able to work up enough courage to do so.

Andrea's laugh rippled through the air, and Liz glanced back at them again to see what was so funny.

Andrea had her hand on Gabriel's arm and seemed to be laughing at something he'd just said. The way the female agent was smiling at Gabriel looked flirtatious… but that couldn't be true, could it? Andrea had made it clear she had no interest in Gabriel. Unless that had changed over the past few days? Liz took a steadying breath and walked over to where they stood.

"What's so funny?"

Andrea looked over at her and smiled. "Gabriel just challenged me to see who would make it to the summit first. He thinks I'll drop back and have to rest while he goes right on up that mountain. But he's wrong. I reminded him that I ran the Yellow Brick Road at the academy in record time. In fact, I think I beat his time."

Liz looked from Andrea to Gabriel. "The Yellow Brick Road? What's that?"

"It's a six-mile obstacle course at the FBI training center. It's the final physical exam at the end of the course, and I aced it." Andrea lifted her chin high as she finished.

Gabriel chuckled. "Well, we'll see how you make it with the llamas."

Andrea sighed and surveyed the eight llamas that stood patiently waiting beside the trail. "Yeah, that's the only downer. I'll just have to keep my distance."

"Llamas bother you, too?" Liz asked.

"Not as much as horses, but yeah. I'm just really not an animal person. Especially any animal big enough to trample me if it felt like it."

At that moment the llama wrangler came around the side of the trailer that he'd used to transport the animals to the trailhead. He walked over to where they stood and stuck out his hand. "I don't think I told you my name when we first arrived. I'm Jeff, and I've been the wrangler with these llamas for about five years now. They're really gentle animals, so you don't need to worry about them."

Gabriel shook his hand and then Andrea and Liz did, too. "Thanks for taking us up the mountain, Jeff," Gabriel said. "None of us are experienced hikers, and we don't know the trails around here. I'm glad we have you to guide us."

Jeff nodded. "No problem. I go up three times a week. We take food and clean laundry up and bring down anything that needs to go."

Liz admired the animals standing quietly beside the trailer and smiled. "Gabriel said that mules used to do the job but they weren't really suited to mountain trails like llamas."

"That's right. And the mules' hooves did a lot of damage to the trail. These guys are built for the job. They're sure-footed, and they can carry up to 35 percent of their weight up a trail. The best part is they are gentle and work for pancakes."

Liz's eyebrows rose. "Pancakes?"

Jeff laughed. "Yeah, that's what the folks at the summit feed them when we get there. Pancakes."

"Sounds like I'm going to get along with these fellows better than I ever did with a horse." Andrea shot a glance in the llamas' direction before she turned back to Jeff. "How long will it take us to get there?"

Jeff tugged on the bill of the Atlanta Braves baseball cap he wore and pulled it lower on his forehead. "There are five trails going up the mountain, but I always use the Trillium Gap Trail. It's a little longer than the others, but the climb isn't as steep. We're going about seven miles up the mountain. It usually takes me about four hours."

Gabriel propped his hands on his hips and stared up the trail. "I suppose you make some rest stops along the way."

"Yeah. I'll have to water the animals. But if you folks need to stop, let me know, and we will. So are you ready to start?"

Gabriel looked at Andrea and then at her. "Ready?"

They both nodded, and he turned back to Jeff. "Lead the way. We'll bring up the rear." He turned to Andrea. "I'll follow behind the llamas. Liz, you follow me, and, Andrea, you bring up the rear."

Before Liz could ask any questions, he whirled and walked over to where Jeff was getting the pack train spread out for their ascent. Then when the animals appeared ready to go, Jeff led the way onto the trail. Gabriel followed the pack train, but he didn't look back.

Liz watched him walk away from her and wondered what had happened that had caused the shift in Gabriel's attitude toward her. Had she done something wrong? Could she fix things between them? Or was she better off letting him pull away, since they didn't have long before the assignment would end, anyway? But even if he headed to Texas after the Shaw trial and she never saw him again, she still didn't like the thought of their friendship ending on such a cold and distant note.

After the night they'd talked in the kitchen, they'd grown closer as they'd worked together in the barn. Now he seemed like a total stranger. Andrea caught up beside her and put her hand on Liz's arm. "Is something the matter?"

She stared at Gabriel's back as he headed up the trail. "I don't know. It's almost like Gabriel's avoiding me. Do you know if I've done something to offend him?"

Andrea's hand stroked Liz's arm, and she spoke in a soothing voice. "I tried to warn you, Liz. I told you Gabriel tires easily of one woman. I've seen it happen a lot of times with him."

Tears filled Liz's eyes, and she turned her head to stare at Andrea. "But we were only friends. What did I do that made him suddenly decide to ignore me?"

Andrea shrugged and gave her an understanding nod. "You didn't do anything, Liz. It's just the way he is. It's better you find out now. He could hurt you worse later."

Liz took a gulp of air and straightened her shoulders. "You're right. I'm better off knowing now." If he was willing to discard their friendship that easily, then she was better off without it. "Now let's get to Mount LeConte."

Andrea smiled. "I'm with you." She reached out and stopped Liz as she began to pull ahead. "And, Liz, remember that I'm here to help you if I can. I feel like we've become friends in the last few weeks, and it tears me up to see you hurt like this."

She patted Andrea's hand. "Don't worry about me. I'm fine. The only thing I should be worrying about right now is staying alive so I can testify in court."

Andrea smiled. "That's right. Even if you do sense Gabriel has distanced himself from you, he would never let anything happen to you. He hasn't failed in an assignment yet, and he doesn't intend to in this one."

So she really was only an assignment to him after all. How could she have been so stupid as to have started to care for a man who saw her only as the next case that would help him climb the ladder to his dream job?

Just a few more weeks, and then she would testify. After that, she never wanted to see Gabriel Decker again.

Gabriel fought the urge to look behind him as he trudged up the trail. He wondered how Liz was making the climb, but Andrea would alert him if there was a problem. So far everything seemed to be going well.

His thoughts were interrupted by Jeff, who called over his shoulder, "Grotto Falls is just ahead. We've come about a mile from the trailhead, and it's our first small obstacle. Tell the ladies to be careful. The trail goes behind the falls, and the rocks get slippery at times. If everybody watches their step, they'll be okay."

Gabriel paused and waited for Liz and Andrea to catch up. He couldn't take his eyes off Liz as she came closer, her hands clasped around the walking sticks that propelled her along. She had her head down and didn't realize he'd stopped until she'd almost plowed into him. A startled look flashed in her eyes when she saw him, and she came to an abrupt halt.

"Sorry. I wasn't watching where I was going."

He only nodded and waited for Andrea. When she'd

joined them, he told them what Jeff had said. "So be careful on the rocks. We don't need any injuries." He looked at Liz. "Do you think you'll need any help navigating the path?"

Her eyes cast a steely look at him, and she shook her head. "You don't have to worry about me. I can hold my own on this hike."

She spit the words at him as if they were distasteful, and he almost reeled from the surprise. What was up with her? He'd never heard her use such an acid tone with anyone before. It was as if some other woman had suddenly inhabited her body. All he could do was bob his head. "Okay. Just asking."

He turned and walked toward the llama train that was now making its way along the rock wall behind the waterfall. He waited as the animals filed underneath the water that poured from above. They didn't seem to mind the roaring sound of the falls or the slippery rocks.

At the moment he wasn't concerned about those things either. He was too focused on trying to figure out why Liz had snapped at him. But none of the answers he could think of made sense. For right now, though, the most important thing was keeping her safe, and he intended to do that. Maybe he should have told her about Gene Curtis's death, but he and Dean had decided she hadn't gotten over nearly dying in the workshop. He'd failed her that day when he didn't go to the barn as soon as he had the feeling something was wrong. He had no plans to fail her again.

In addition to keeping alert to protect Liz, he had another big problem on his mind. He'd been thinking about the things Dean had said to him at the hospital, and he'd been reading the Bible that Liz had given him. But he didn't know whether he'd ever be able to believe like they did. He still couldn't rationalize this thing called faith.

It wasn't fair to think about trying to pursue a relationship with Liz when their beliefs were so far apart. Sooner or later she'd come to grow tired of the constant struggle, and she'd leave him. Maybe it wouldn't be at the altar, but she would leave. He didn't think he could survive that again.

Maybe being on a mountaintop would give him time to sort out his feelings and decide which path he needed to take. He knew he was incredibly drawn to Liz, but he wasn't sure she needed a man like him who had no faith in anything. And the question of whether or not she returned his feelings would be a moot point if he didn't keep her safe.

Jeff called out to him, and he noticed that the llamas had made it to the other side of the stream and were waiting placidly on the bank. He waved at Jeff and began his crossing. As he walked behind the waterfall, he felt the spray hitting the rocks around him and bouncing onto him. With careful steps he made his way forward and finally reached the bank beside the pack train.

He turned to see Liz moving across the narrow path. She had almost reached the stream's bank when her foot slipped on a moss-covered rock, and she lunged forward. Gabriel grabbed for her, caught her just before she fell, wrapping his arms around her.

For an instant all he wanted was to hold her forever. The scent of her shampoo wafted to his nose, and he tightened his grip on her. This was what he wanted. This was where she needed to be. In his arms.

"Are you okay?" he whispered.

Her body, which had been so relaxed against his, suddenly stiffened, and she pushed against his hold on her. He had no choice except to release her. She straightened to her full height and stared at him as if she didn't know him.

"I'm fine. Thank you for catching me."

Then she brushed past him and walked after the pack train, which was now continuing on its journey. He stared after her for a moment and then turned to Andrea, who had just completed the crossing.

"Ready to go?" she asked.

He nodded. "You take the lead with Liz for a while. I'll hang back."

She didn't say anything as she increased her stride and got in front of Liz. He stood on the stream's bank and watched them go before he sighed and followed after them. From the way this trip had started off, it wasn't difficult to predict what the next few weeks were going to be like. The autumn winds up here on the mountain couldn't be any colder than the frosty look Liz had directed at him. It looked like they were in for a bumpy ride.

An hour after leaving Grotto Falls, they came to a place where the rushing mountain stream forked. In one spot the water rippled over the rocks in its bed. Gabriel had never seen anything quite so peaceful.

"This is where I water the llamas," Jeff told them, and the animals began to crowd toward the stream as if they understood what he'd said.

Gabriel watched in wonder as the llamas quietly drank and then raised their heads to survey their surroundings. Liz sank down on a big rock beside the stream and pulled a bottle of water from her backpack. She took a drink, then looked up to find him staring at her.

He quickly averted his eyes and scanned the area. Suddenly his gaze locked on a man who knelt on the ground a few feet away from where Liz sat. His hands shook as he dipped a canteen into the water.

Other than the way his body appeared to be trembling, there was something else about the man's appearance that caught his attention. He didn't have a backpack, which made him look out of place on the mountain trail.

Gabriel's suspicions escalated as he let his gaze wander over the man's long hair, which was pulled back in a ponytail, the black plugs that pierced his ears and the full beard that didn't quite cover the scar that ran from his chin to his ear. All these things taken as a whole gave off a sinister look that made his skin prickle.

As he was watching, he saw Liz approach the man. Before he could call out to her, she stopped, bent over and smiled down at the man.

"You're not going to drink that, are you?" she asked.

Her voice seemed to startle him, and he lost his grip on the canteen. He caught it just before it hit the water and looked up at her. "Excuse me?"

Her smile grew larger. "I said you aren't going to drink that, are you?"

He frowned. "I was planning to. Do you have a problem with that?"

She squatted down next to him so that they were on the same eye level. "Well, actually, I do. You can't believe what you hear about the water in mountain streams being pure. It's really contaminated from all the pollution. You may get sick if you drink that."

He shrugged. "You do what you have to do."

She glanced around. "Where's your backpack?"

"Almost down the mountain by this time, I guess."

Liz's eyebrows arched. "I don't understand."

The man sighed as if he wished she'd leave him alone, but he turned to stare at her. "I was on my way up the mountain when I stopped here to rest. Two guys were coming down, and they sat down with me. Something hit me in the head, and I blacked out. When I woke up, I discovered they'd stolen my backpack and everything else I had except this small canteen on my belt. So I'm filling it to have something to drink on the rest of the climb."

"Oh, I'm so sorry." Her voice held a soothing tone. "Do you need me to look at your head?"

"Naw, that's okay. It's just a small cut."

"Well, you need to notify the sheriff and the park officials when you get back down."

His eyes grew wide. "Why would I do that?"

"To file a report so the men can be arrested."

He looked at her as if he couldn't believe what she was saying. "No need to involve the police—I'll make them pay. I remember some things about them that are gonna help me track them down."

Liz didn't say anything for a moment, and then she took a deep breath. "So are you going back down now?"

"Naw, I got things to do at the top. I reckon I'll just go on."

"But if you don't have any supplies, why don't you just go back down?"

He shot a glance at Gabriel as if to beg him to make her stop pestering him with questions, but Gabriel was now too interested in the rest of the story. "Because I'm meeting people there and if I don't show up, my friends will get upset. And when they get upset, it ain't a pretty sight. All the rangers in this part of the park will be out all night searching for me. Besides, they'll let me share their stuff when I get there."

Liz frowned and nodded as the man put the canteen back in the water. Suddenly his body jerked, and he sat back on his heels. Liz grabbed his arm. "What's wrong?"

"Diabetic," he said through clenched teeth. "Blood sugar dropping."

Gabriel and Andrea both jumped to their feet, but Liz was faster. She grabbed her backpack, got it unzipped and had a chocolate candy bar shoved in the man's hands before they could cover the distance to where she sat.

"Eat this," she commanded.

The man's eyes blinked rapidly as he stared at Liz. When he didn't respond, she broke off a piece of the candy and forced it into his mouth. As if on autopilot he began to chew and then swallowed the bite. He opened his mouth as if to speak, and she pushed another chunk of chocolate into his mouth. Gabriel watched in fascination as she continued to feed the man. As she did, the color in his face gradually returned and replaced the pale, ashen skin tone of a few minutes earlier. The shakiness he'd shown earlier settled, too.

Liz laid her hand on his shoulder. "How are you feeling now?"

He eyed her. "Better. Thanks." The words held a grudging tone.

She sat back on her heels and smiled. "You're welcome. My father was a diabetic, and I had to feed him candy many times." She reached in her backpack again and pulled out a bottle of water. "Empty that canteen and drink this instead."

He faltered for a second and then took the bottle. "You don't have to do more, Miss..."

"Liz," she finished for him. "And you are?"

"Brick."

Liz smiled. "Well, it's nice to meet you, Brick."

He didn't respond as he raised his head and took a swig from the bottle. As he did, the tattoo on the side of his neck came into full view—a skull, the symbol of a vicious gang the FBI had been trying to take down for years.

Gabriel couldn't pry his eyes off the tattoo. When he finally glanced up, his gaze locked with Brick's. The man was frowning as if he knew exactly what Gabriel was thinking. They stared at each other for a few seconds before Brick looked away.

"Hey," Jeff called from the front of the pack train. "It's time to go. You folks ready?"

Gabriel picked up his backpack. The sooner they got away from this guy, the better. "Let's go, Liz."

She zipped her pack up and slung it over her shoulder. "Are you up to walking yet, Brick?"

He nodded. "Yeah. Maybe I'll see you on top."

She raised her eyebrows. "We're not leaving you here."

Gabriel had already taken a step toward Jeff, and he spun around. "Liz, I really don't think…"

"He can't go on alone. He might have another attack, and there'd be nobody to help. Besides, we have water, and he doesn't." She looked down at Brick, who stared up at her. "So on your feet, Brick. It's time to get moving."

He pushed to a standing position and grimaced. "I'll be okay. I don't…"

She held her palm out facing him and shook her head. "No arguments. I'm not leaving you here by yourself. So you might as well come on."

Gabriel started to protest again, but Andrea touched his arm. "Leave it alone, Gabriel. You can't change her mind."

He looked back to where Liz had been a moment ago, but she had Brick by the arm and was leading him over to where Jeff and the llamas waited. Gabriel gritted his teeth. "All right, but did you see that tattoo?"

"I did, but it's better that we have him close so we can keep an eye on him."

"Then you go in front of her, and I'll bring up the rear in case he tries something."

Andrea trotted off and took up her position in front of Liz as the pack train began to move. Liz had treated that guy just the way she did Bart Foster. Did she not realize the danger these men posed? The Piranhas and the Skulls inhabited the same world that Daniel Shaw lived in, and their members would be the perfect choice to perform a hit for him.

Brick might have gotten sympathy from Liz, but he'd get none from Gabriel. In fact, as long as they were on the mountain, he was going to keep the gang member and his friends on his radar.

ELEVEN

Two hours later the Mount LeConte Lodge with its cabins came into view. Liz had never been as thankful to see any sight in her life. Even with the rest stops they'd taken along the way, the climb had been strenuous, and at times she wasn't sure she'd make it. Then she'd glance at Andrea, who was striding along like she did a seven-mile hike every morning before breakfast, and she'd push herself to show Andrea and Gabriel that she could keep up.

Brick had made it fine, too. He hadn't talked much on the way to the lodge, but she'd found out a few things. He'd grown up in a rough neighborhood in Memphis and had been on his own since he was sixteen. He mentioned his friends several times, and she sensed they were more than just friends, closer to family really. When she had asked him if they were staying at the lodge, he'd shaken his head and said they were staying in a backcountry shelter close by.

Gabriel hadn't been happy that she'd insisted Brick come along, but she couldn't leave him on the mountain alone. Besides, it didn't matter what Gabriel thought. She was beginning to see a side to him that she didn't like. He'd spoken to her only in short sentences since they'd left the trailhead.

Brick seemed to sense her exhaustion as they neared the lodge, and he pointed to the building about four hundred feet away. "There's the office. I see my friends on the front porch."

She squinted to get a better look at the building and spied two men sitting in rocking chairs outside the front door. As they continued toward them, the men stood, came down the steps and watched as the llama pack train got closer.

They exchanged somber glances before they turned and gazed at Gabriel, then Andrea, then her. Her skin prickled at the sense of danger that seemed to surround them. She'd never felt a sensation like that in her life upon first seeing someone, and she stepped a little closer to Brick.

When they reached the stairs, Jeff nodded to the strangers but kept walking as he led the llamas around to the back door. The two men glanced at Gabriel once more and then fastened their eyes on Brick as they approached. "What's this?" one of them asked.

Brick gave a curt nod of acknowledgment. "Had a little problem on the trail. Tell you about it later. This lady helped me out."

Up close the men looked even more sinister. They each had long hair that was pulled back in a ponytail, and the older one had a beard that hung down to his chest. They wore T-shirts, but she could see tattoos that curled up their arms.

At Brick's words, both men shifted their attention to her. "That so?"

"Yes," Liz answered. "I'm afraid he's had a rough time. You need to make sure you have a good supply of candy while you're here."

The one with the long beard looked back at Brick. "You have a problem with your sugar level?"

Brick nodded. "Yeah. I guess I'd be passed out in the woods if it wasn't for this lady. She forced candy in my mouth. Then she gave me her water so I wouldn't have to drink from the stream and wouldn't leave until I came with her."

The man's hand stroked his beard as he studied her for a minute. "You don't say."

"Yeah. I'll tell you about it later. Let's go."

The bearded man stuck out his hand, and Liz put hers in it. His big fingers wrapped around hers, and then he covered her hand with his other one. "My name is Clipper." He indicated the other man. "And this is Patch. I'm much obliged to you for you taking care of my brother."

Surprised, Liz looked around at Brick. "Brother? I thought you were meeting friends."

The two men chuckled. "Friends that are really brothers," Clipper said.

Just then Gabriel walked up beside her, took hold of her arm and tugged it free. "We need to check in."

Liz frowned up at him. "You go on and take care of that. I'm going to sit down in that rocking chair and rest." She faced Brick again. "That is, after I say good-bye to Brick and his brothers."

Brick glowered at Gabriel and glanced back at his friends. "Let's go."

He started to leave, and Liz called after him. "Take care of yourself."

He looked back at her. "I will. You do the same."

With those words, the three men turned and headed up the path that led to a line of trees farther up the mountain. When they'd disappeared, Gabriel turned to her, and she couldn't quite determine the look on his face. Irritation or fear?

She gulped and raised her chin. "I thought you needed to check in."

"Liz, that was a reckless thing to do."

She wrinkled her forehead. "What are you talking about?"

"Those guys, Brick and his friends. You need to stay away from them."

She tilted her head to one side and studied Gabriel's face. "Why?"

"Didn't you see their tattoos?"

"Well, yes, but I've seen tattoos before."

The muscle in his jaw flexed, and he took a step closer to her. "You haven't seen those kind before. They're not just decoration. Brick and his friends are members of a motorcycle gang in Memphis called the Skulls. We've been after them for years. In fact, I think they recognized me."

Liz arched her eyebrows. "So what has the FBI proven against them so far?"

"Well, nothing yet, but that doesn't mean we won't. You should never have helped that guy on the trail."

She couldn't believe he'd said that. She frowned and propped her hands on her hips. "Not helped him? Gabriel, we are all God's children, and He loves us all the same. I would be denying what God wants me to do if I turned my back and ignored a man when it was apparent he was in distress. Especially when I knew I had the tools to help. I believe that God expects us to help those in trouble no matter who they are."

He clenched his teeth at her. "Even if they might be here to carry out a hit?" He stopped and pushed his hand through his hair. "Now I've got one more thing to worry about."

Before she could respond, he stormed up the steps and disappeared into the office. Exhausted, Liz watched him go and then climbed the stairs and sank down in the rocking chair. She laid her head against the high back of the chair and closed her eyes.

The things Gabriel said troubled her, but she wouldn't have done anything differently with Brick if she'd known about his gang affiliation. Though he hadn't exactly been friendly, he'd been polite all the way up the mountain, and he'd seemed to be sincere in his appreciation for what she'd done. She'd lived her life believing that there was some good in everyone, and her short encounter with Brick had led her to think that there was some in him, too.

Her eyes still shut, she smiled at the cool fall breeze that blew across her face. She didn't know if she'd ever want to get out of this chair. Her reprieve was short-lived because Gabriel was back within minutes with directions to their cabin. "We're just up the path from the dining room. Come on."

He bounded down the steps and headed up the rocky path, but Andrea, who'd followed her to the porch, bent down over her. "Are you okay, Liz?"

"Just a little tired. It feels so good to sit down. Now that I have, I don't think I'm ever going to be able to move."

"Then sit there and rest for a few minutes. I'm going in the office to see if they have snacks for sale. I'll be right back."

A contented sigh escaped from Liz's mouth, and she leaned back into the chair. The door to the office opened, and Liz's eyes popped open. A man dressed in shorts and a T-shirt walked out. A backpack hung over his shoulder.

When he saw her in the chair, he stopped and smiled. "Hello. Are you just getting here?"

"Yes. How about you?"

He set his backpack down on the porch and wiped the sweat from his forehead. "Me, too. I didn't see you on the trail. Did you come up the Alum Cave Trail?"

She shook her head. "No. We did the Trillium Gap Trail."

He smiled. "I did that one when I hiked up here in the middle of the summer. It's really a beautiful hike." He stuck out his hand. "By the way, I'm Frank. And you are?"

"Liz."

"It's good to meet you, Liz. Are you staying at the lodge or at one of the backcountry shelters?"

"Here at the lodge. I have a cabin."

He sighed. "I wish I could say the same, but I couldn't get one. Im staying at one of the backcountry shelters." He nodded toward the door. "I was just talking to the people in there, and they said I could eat here tonight. So that's good."

"Then maybe I'll see you at dinner."

His gaze raked her face, and he smiled. "I'd like that."

Liz didn't get a chance to respond because an angry voice cut in. "I wondered where you had gone to." They turned as Gabriel came up the steps to the porch. A frown pulled at his forehead. "I thought you were right behind me."

Liz rolled her eyes and leveled an exasperated gaze at him. "Take it easy, Gabriel. I was just talking with a fellow camper. This is Frank."

Gabriel gave the man a curt nod. "Good to meet you."

Frank offered his hand, and Gabriel took it. Liz could tell from the set of his jaw that he did it reluctantly. "Are you Liz's husband?" Frank asked.

Liz laughed before she realized it. "Husband? No. We're just friends. We're here with our other friend, Andrea."

Frank raised an eyebrow. "Oh, I see." He picked up his backpack, took Liz's hand in his and held it for a moment. "In that case, I'll make it a point to see you at dinner."

With that, he hopped down the steps and strode down the trail away from the cabins. Gabriel watched him, then turned back to Liz. "What is it with you? Are you determined to meet every guy who's hiked up Mount LeConte today?'

Liz bit down on her tongue as she shoved to her feet and glared at Gabriel. "What's that supposed to mean?"

"First Brick and his friends, and now Frank. Do you not realize that we're here to keep you safe? How can we do that if you attract the attention of every male in a ten-mile radius?"

She balled her fists at her sides and stepped closer. "I've only tried to be nice. It might not hurt you to do the same thing every once in a while."

His jaw ticked as he ran his hand through his hair. "Liz, you are driving me crazy. I…" The he stopped. "Never mind. Where is Andrea?"

"She went inside to see about getting some snacks."

"Snacks?" Gabriel exploded. "And left you alone out here?"

Now his face had turned red, and his eyes burned like a fire. She could tell he was about to completely lose it. She moved toward him. "Would you calm down?" she hissed. "I thought you wanted to avoid drawing attention to us. Besides, you don't need to broadcast it to everyone in camp that I have a babysitter."

His eyes got big. "Babysitter? Do you think that's what I am?'

"No, that's what *you* think you are. I'm just another assignment, one that's going to help you get that promotion you're looking for."

The angry expression faded as his jaw slackened and

he shook his head. "How could you think that about me?" he whispered.

"With the way you've been acting, it doesn't take a genius to figure out that you can't wait for this assignment to be over." Her heart lurched at the hurt she saw in his eyes, and she wanted to throw her arms around him and beg him to forgive her for the things she'd said. Instead she picked up her backpack and gestured toward the office. "Why don't you get Andrea, and let's get settled."

For a second he stood completely still. Then he gave a slow nod and stepped around her. He returned right away with Andrea. He didn't say a word as he strode down the steps and started up the path.

"What happened?" Andrea whispered.

Liz watched Gabriel's straight back and long strides as he headed toward the cabin. "Nothing important."

She wanted to rush after him, but she didn't think he wanted to talk to her right now.

Her pulse pounded in her ears, and she took several slow breaths to calm herself. Tears pooled in her eyes. All she'd wanted that day months ago was to get away for the weekend with her best friend, and it had led to a sequence of events that now found her staring at the man she'd started to care for as he walked away from her.

Had she just imagined that he enjoyed being with her? Had it been only a ruse so that she would allow him to stay close and protect her? If so, he'd played his part well and had her convinced he really liked her.

Now he acted like she was a stranger, just another

woman that he'd tired of and was ready to free himself from, as Andrea had implied was his usual practice. If that's what he wanted, there was nothing she could do about it. You couldn't make someone love you. This was just one more loss that she was going to have to deal with.

She gulped down another deep breath. She'd faced a lot of disappointments and heartaches in the last few years, and through it all, she'd discovered the secret to survival. It was her faith, and it wouldn't let her down this time. The future might look uncertain at the moment, but God would help her get through the dark days ahead.

What she had to do right now was concentrate on the trial. That was the important thing. She couldn't allow anything to sidetrack her from getting justice for Kathy. Once that was over, she would decide what she wanted to do with the rest of her life. Until then she couldn't let thoughts of Gabriel distract her. She just couldn't.

The atmosphere in the cabin had been like a deep freeze all afternoon. When he and Liz had entered the cottage, she'd headed into the bedroom she and Andrea would be sharing and closed the door. He considered knocking and asking her to explain the things she'd said outside the office, but instead he turned and entered the smaller bedroom where he would be sleeping.

A few minutes later he heard Andrea come in. She'd also gone into their bedroom, and that's where she and Liz had stayed until it was time to go to dinner. Now they sat in the dining room with all the other mountaintop guests.

Andrea had kept up a lively conversation all during the meal, but Liz had stayed silent. Every now and then she glanced at him but she always averted her eyes when she caught him looking at her. Exasperated with her attitude, he surveyed the rustic dining room. It reminded him of something you would see in a movie about life in the mountains in the days before electricity.

Wooden dining tables, each with six ladder-back chairs, lined the walls. Servers moved along the long narrow walkway down the middle of the room, but it was the presence of flickering oil lamps on the tables and attached to the walls that gave the room a rustic feeling. The tired voices of the guests who'd spent a day hiking Mount LeConte echoed all around him, but he couldn't keep his attention off Liz.

He suddenly realized that Andrea was waving her open palm in front of his face. "Earth to Gabriel. Come in, please."

Startled from his thoughts, he pulled his gaze to her. "Did you say something?"

"Yes, I said it's a little chilly in here. I think I'll run back to the cabin and get my sweater. It won't take but a few minutes. Then I'll finish dinner. Can I get anything for either of you?"

Liz shook her head but didn't look up from a bowl of beef stew in front of her.

What was the matter with Liz that she couldn't even look him in the eye? He didn't remember doing anything to anger her, but ever since she'd gotten out of the hospital, she'd treated him like he had some kind of terrible disease she was trying to avoid.

"Nothing for me, either," he finally said.

Andrea scooted her chair away from the table and jumped to her feet. "Then I'll be back before you know it."

With her departure the silence only deepened at the table. He couldn't take much more of this. His fork rattled when he dropped it to his plate, and some people at the next table looked up. But he didn't care. It was time he put a stop to whatever was going on.

"Liz…" He only got her name out before he sensed someone standing next to the table. He glanced up and into the face of the man they'd met on the office porch earlier.

"Well, we meet again." He smiled down at them and let his gaze go from Gabriel to Liz. "It's good to see you."

Liz looked up and smiled. "Hello, Frank."

Andrea's food still sat at the place next to him, but the chair next to Liz was vacant. Frank glanced at it. "I haven't had dinner yet, and yours are the only familiar faces I see in the place. Would you folks mind if I joined you?"

Gabriel was about to decline, but before he could respond, Liz indicated the empty chair. "Sure. Have a seat next to me."

Frank was moving toward the seat almost before she had finished the sentence. "Thanks. I've spent so much time alone in the mountains this summer that it'll be good to enjoy a meal with some conversation."

The young woman who'd been serving their table came over just then, and Frank listened to her as she recited the night's special. Gabriel studied the man as he listened and gave her his order. He looked harmless enough, a little geeky really, with his dark-rimmed glasses and hair that appeared to not have been cut in a while.

When the server left the table, Frank smiled at Liz. "You told me this afternoon that you came up the Trillium Gap Trail. Did you enjoy the climb?"

She nodded. "I really did. I'm not much of a hiker, but we came up with the llama train and that proved interesting."

Frank laughed. "I can imagine. They're amazing creatures." He glanced at Gabriel. "And how about you? Do you hike a lot?"

"Some." Gabriel paused. "So, Frank, you said you've spent a lot of time in the mountains. You must be an avid hiker."

Frank shook his head. "Not really. I'm a botanist. I've spent all summer trekking around the mountains and checking out the wildflowers here. Now that fall is here, it's time for me to return home."

"And where's home?" Gabriel asked.

"Knoxville. I teach at the University of Tennessee, and classes start next week. So my time here is coming to a close." He sighed and shook his head. "I really hate to leave. These hills are a virtual paradise for plant lovers."

Liz swiveled in her chair and regarded him. "You must have seen a lot of the backcountry this summer."

"I have, and it's an experience that I will never forget. I have no idea how many miles I've hiked, how many people I've met or how many native wildflowers I've cataloged, but it's been a summer I'll never forget."

Gabriel felt a pang of jealousy when he saw that Liz was hanging on every word Frank said. He pushed his plate away and crossed his arms on top of the table. "So, Frank, I don't believe I caught your last name."

The server arrived then with Frank's food, and he waited until it was on the table in front of him before he responded. "Myers. Dr. Frank Myers."

"And you teach at UT?"

Frank had just shoveled a spoonful of beef stew in his mouth, and he swallowed before answering. "Yes. I teach two classes in plant sciences and two in ecology. I've been on sabbatical for the past year, and I'm looking forward to getting back into the classroom."

Gabriel tried to stem his growing feeling of wariness for Frank. Okay, so the man lived in Knoxville, not Memphis, and he seemed to have no criminal connections—but that didn't mean Gabriel was ready to trust him. Could it be that he was a bit angry because Liz seemed to fascinated by what he had to say? He wished he had some way of checking him out.

As if in answer to his wish, Andrea came back into the dining room. When she saw Frank at the table, she flicked a quick glance at Gabriel before she slid into her seat. "Hello," she said. "I don't think we've met. My name is Andrea."

He reached across the table and shook her hand. "It's good to meet you, Andrea. I'm Frank."

Gabriel shoved his chair back and stood. "If you'll excuse me, I need to do something. I'll be back in a few minutes."

Liz and Andrea both gave him questioning looks, but Frank appeared too busy devouring the food on his plate to note the tension. Gabriel tried not to hurry as he walked to the door that led to the front of the building. When he stepped outside, it seemed that the night enveloped him in the dark. With no electric lights, it was difficult to see much of anything.

He pulled his cell phone and the flashlight he'd brought with him to the dining room from his pockets, backed up against the wall of the building and sighed in relief when he saw that he had cell service. He navigated to the internet and to the University of Tennessee website. It took him only a few minutes to find Frank Myers listed as a teacher of plant sciences. There was no picture, but it did say he was presently on sabbatical.

Gabriel ended the connection and slipped his phone back in his pocket. He had become paranoid. He saw danger everywhere he turned. Maybe that's why Liz had suddenly seemed to take a dislike to him.

He opened the door and walked back into the dining room. Just as he did, he heard Liz's laugh ring out, and he glanced at the table where she sat. She and Andrea both seemed engrossed in what Frank was saying.

He watched her for a moment before he headed over to the table and stopped beside her. "I'm tired. I think I'll go back to the cabin. Can you walk Liz back, Andrea?"

"Sure. I even have my flashlight. You go on. We'll be there in a bit."

He waited to see if Liz would ask him to stay or offer to walk back with him. When she didn't, he sighed. "Okay. I'll see you later."

Gabriel didn't look back as he left the dining room and started up the trail to their cabin. When he stepped up onto the small porch, he dropped down in one of the rocking chairs that sat there. He folded his hands across his stomach, leaned his head back and closed his eyes.

It had been a long day, and he was tired. But he was not only physically tired, he was sick and tired of the way Liz was acting. For some reason a problem had erupted between them, and he didn't know what it was. One thing he did know, however—he was going to sit on this porch until she got home. Then he'd make her explain what had made things go so awry between them. And he wasn't giving up until she told him the truth.

TWELVE

Liz tried to act interested in what Frank was saying, but her mind kept returning to how Gabriel had looked when he'd come back to the table. He really did seem tired. Maybe he was getting sick. She chewed her lower lip. She didn't need to be thinking about him right now. She should concentrate on Frank and Andrea and the conversation they appeared to be engaged in.

The door opened, and Liz's gaze turned in that direction. She smiled when she saw Brick walk in. He came toward their table and paused next to her. His gaze traveled over Andrea and Frank before he looked down at her. "Hello, Liz."

She smiled up at him. "Hi, Brick. Would you like to sit down with us?"

He glanced at Frank once more and shook his head. "No, thanks. Clipper and Patch will be here in a few minutes. We're just gonna get something real quick and then get on back up to the shelter where we're staying."

"Did your friends have enough supplies to share with you?"

He nodded. "Yeah. I'm fine. You don't need to worry about me. Good to see you."

With that, he turned and walked to an empty table at the back of the room and sat down in one of the chairs facing her. He didn't look up when the server stopped to tell him the special.

After the server had gone back to the kitchen, Liz kept an eye on Brick. He sat at the last table in the room with his back against the far wall. His gaze darted constantly around the room and only paused now and then to stare at something. It was as if he was studying everyone in the place. Every once in a while his eyes would blink and she'd find him staring at her. Then he'd turn his attention to Frank before he looked away.

He was almost through with his meal when Clipper and Patch walked in. They passed by the table where she sat and nodded at her before they took their seats with Brick, who continued to scan the room. The three men leaned over the table, their heads close together, as they whispered for several minutes. Then they glanced back at their table, and cold chills rippled down her spine. She didn't want to believe these men were a threat to her safety…but she couldn't forget Gabriel's warning earlier.

She forced herself to focus on the story Frank was telling about being chased by a bear on the Appalachian Trail earlier in the summer. As he shared the experience, Liz became so caught up in the tale that she didn't look in the men's direction for at least ten minutes. When she did, she was surprised to see that they were gone. How had they walked by the table without her noticing them?

Frank wiped his mouth on his napkin and laid it beside his plate. "Now, I hate to leave, but I want to be out on the trail early in the morning. Thank you for gracing me with your company while I ate."

"It was our pleasure," Andrea said. "Will we see you before you leave?"

"Maybe," he said. "I should be around tomorrow night, but I leave the next day. If you're ever in Knoxville, look me up. You'll usually find me in my office on campus."

"We'll do that." Andrea smiled up at him.

"I hope so," he said before he turned and left.

Liz watched Andrea as she continued to stare at the door even after Frank had gone. She leaned over and whispered, "I think he likes you."

Andrea's face turned crimson, and she straightened in her chair. "He was nice to both of us."

"Then why did I get the impression that his invitation to look him up was meant solely for you?"

Andrea's blush deepened even as she waved her hand in dismissal. "You're wrong." Then a slow smile spread across her face, and she quirked an eyebrow. "But a college professor would sure be a good catch. I may have to look up the good doctor tomorrow."

Liz burst out laughing. "You are so funny, Andrea. I don't know what I would have done if you hadn't been with me the last few weeks. Gabriel doesn't seem to have much of a sense of humor, but you make me laugh a lot."

Andrea glanced at her watch and then pushed to her feet. "Let's go back to the cabin and have a girls' slumber party. I've got stories that will make you laugh even when your hair is standing on end."

Liz chuckled, shook her head and stood up. "I can hardly wait."

They walked out of the dining room into the black night, and Liz stopped briefly to stare up at the overcast sky. No stars or even the moon were visible tonight, and a thick darkness hung over the area. They'd stayed in the dining room longer than anyone else, and now there was no movement anywhere.

"I wonder where everybody is," Liz said.

"Probably inside their cabins and getting ready for bed. These people are hikers. They'll be up with the sun and out on the trails around here. Not us, though. I think we deserve a morning to sleep in."

Liz grinned. "Sounds good to me."

Andrea looped her arm through Liz's. "Even though I aced the Yellow Brick Road at the academy, I really don't care for hiking. That trip up the mountain and the one back down are enough for me."

Liz pulled to a stop and looked at Andrea. "Do you really think I'm safe here?"

Andrea tightened her grip on Liz's arm. "Liz, if I joke around a lot, it's to try to give you peace of mind. Daniel Shaw has contacts everywhere, so we should always be on our guard, but all the same, I believe you're safe here."

"Gabriel is worried about Brick and his friends. He says they're members of a gang."

Andrea nodded. "I didn't know he'd told you that. Yes, they are, but that doesn't mean they're here for you.

Gabriel and I are going to keep a closer watch on you, especially now since Gene…"

She stopped in the middle of the sentence, and Liz's heart plummeted to the pit of her stomach. "Since Gene what?"

Andrea tugged on her arm. "It doesn't matter. Let's go."

Liz dug her heels into the path and refused to move. "It does matter. What were you going to say?"

"Liz, I don't think we should get into this right now."

Liz put her hands on her hips and glared at Andrea even though she was sure that Andrea probably couldn't see her face in the dark. "I want to know what you were about to say. I'm not budging from this spot until you tell me."

Andrea gave a sigh. "Okay, but Gabriel is going to kill me for telling you. While you were in the hospital, a body was found on a mountain trail. It was Gene Curtis—the man who attacked you in the movie theater parking lot."

Liz felt as if she'd suddenly been doused with ice. "Wh-what happened to him?"

"He'd been shot."

She started to say she wouldn't have to worry about him hurting her now, but something else Andrea had said flashed into her mind. "Why do you think Gabriel will be angry with you for telling me?"

"Because he didn't want you to worry about the possibility he'd been taken out by another hit man as punishment for failing in his contract."

Liz thought about this for a moment. "Is that why

we've come to Mount LeConte? Because we're hiding out from another hit man?"

"Yes."

Liz's legs began to tremble, and she thought they might collapse. "Is that why Gabriel has been so distant? Because he's worried?"

Andrea reached out and grabbed Liz's hand. "Don't let that bother you. I think he really likes you, and he's afraid he'll fail to keep you safe. I was honest with you when I told you that he changes girlfriends a lot, but I think this time with you it may be different."

Relief surged through Liz, and she smiled. "Do you really think so?"

"I really do. I think…" Andrea didn't finish. Instead she whirled around, pulled her gun from its holster and held up her hand in warning. "Shhh!" she whispered.

Liz's gaze followed Andrea's, which was directed into the shadows on a path that led to some more cabins at the top of a hill. "What is it?" Liz whispered back.

"I think I hear something. Stay here, and I'll check it out."

Liz reached out to stop Andrea, not wanting to be left alone, but the other woman had already disappeared into the darkness. Suddenly Liz heard a grunt and then the sound of something falling. She stood frozen to the spot, her eyes huge and her heart hammering. "Andrea," she whispered.

No answer.

She swallowed and tried again. "Andrea."

The words were barely out of her mouth before a figure appeared from the darkness headed straight for her. His dark clothes and the ski mask he wore made him blend in with the shadows. He raised his arm, and she caught sight of a knife.

She didn't know what had happened to Andrea, but she had to get out of there. She willed her legs to move, and she turned and ran up the path that led to their cabin. "Gabriel!" she screamed at the top of her voice. "Gabriel!"

Footsteps behind her pounded against the earth, and she knew her pursuer was gaining. She screamed again when she felt his fingers brush her shoulder and then jerk away. She could hear grunts behind her, but she didn't turn around to see what was happening. She ran toward the cabin.

She had to get to Gabriel before another hit man finished the job.

Gabriel didn't realize he'd fallen asleep in the rocking chair, but he must have. He awoke with a jolt, sat up straight and scrubbed his hands over his face. It was getting a little chilly. He hadn't heard Liz and Andrea come in, but maybe he'd wait for them inside, where it was warmer.

He put his hands on the rocker's arms to push himself up, but he tensed at a sound much like a scream that seemed to be coming from near the dining room. Then he heard it clearer.

"Gabriel!" the voice screamed. "Gabriel."

That was Liz's voice. Grabbing the flashlight, he jumped up and bounded along the path that led to the dining room. He'd gone only a few feet when Liz plowed into him with such force that it almost knocked him down. He wrapped his arms around her waist as he staggered backward.

She threw her arms around his neck. "Gabriel! Something's happened to Andrea. And somebody attacked me with a knife," she screamed.

He directed the flashlight beam down the path with one hand and pulled out his gun with the other. Then he moved in front of her. "Stay behind me."

With Liz trailing him, Gabriel retraced her steps toward the dining room. He swept his gun back and forth across the path as they walked, but there was no one on the trail. They were just a short distance from the dining room when a low moan reached his ears.

Liz raised a shaking finger and pointed into the darkness. "In there. That's where Andrea went."

Gabriel stopped and peered into the shadows, but he could see nothing. "Andrea, where are you?"

The only answer was another weak moan.

Gabriel tensed and tightened his grip on his gun. "Andrea!"

"H-here."

Gabriel took a few steps, and his foot touched her leg. He squinted, and he could make out her form on the ground. He squatted down and felt for her arm. "Are you hurt?"

She shook her head. "No. I think someone must have knocked me out. My head is pounding."

Liz knelt on the other side of her. "Can you stand up?"

"I—I think so."

Gabriel grabbed one arm, and Liz grabbed the other. Together they helped Andrea to her feet. She swayed back and forth in front of them for a second, then seemed to get her balance.

"What happened?" Liz asked. "I heard sounds like scuffling and then a moan. The next thing I knew, a figure holding a knife was coming at me, so I ran. He almost had hold of my shoulder, and then he pulled away. I heard some more noises behind me, but I kept running and called out for you."

Gabriel scanned the area, but he couldn't make out anyone around. If they were there, they'd hidden themselves well in the darkness. He took Andrea by the arm again. "Let's get you back to the cabin."

He got on one side of her and Liz on the other as they guided her back along the path. When they got inside, Gabriel directed the beam of the flashlight into the darkened cabin as he led her to a chair. He motioned for her to sit. "As soon as I get the oil lamps lit, I want to take a look at your head."

Andrea winced as she eased to the chair. She put her hand to the top of her head and felt her scalp. "I don't feel any cuts."

Gabriel didn't say anything as he removed the chimney from the lamp on the table next to Andrea and touched a match to the wick. When the flame illuminated the room, he ran his fingers over her head. She cringed once when he touched a spot at the back of her head. "Is that tender?"

Andrea nodded. "A bit, but not too bad."

When Gabriel had finished his inspection, he stepped

back and looked down at Andrea. "I think we need to let a doctor look at you."

She chuckled. "Well, have fun trying to find one on top of a mountain late at night."

"Is there anything I can do for you?" Liz asked.

Andrea shook her head. "I'm sorry, Liz. I've been so consumed with my encounter in the dark I haven't asked about you. Are you okay?"

Liz nodded. "Yes. I don't know what happened. Someone was after me—then suddenly he wasn't. It was like something picked him up and threw him away."

Andrea glanced at Gabriel. "Do you have any idea what happened?"

"No. I couldn't find any evidence of anybody being around. Of course, it was dark. I'll take another look when it gets light out."

She pushed to her feet. "Well, wake me if you need me to help you. But for now, I think I need to go to bed."

Liz gasped. "You can't go to sleep. I've always heard that people who've experienced a blow to the head should be kept awake for at least six hours."

Andrea smiled. "That's an old wives' tale. Studies now recommend that a person who's been hit in the head get sleep to recover."

Gabriel cast a skeptical look at Andrea. "Are you sure about that?"

"I'm positive. Now I'm going to bed." She glanced from one to the other. "I think the two of you need to talk and straighten out a few things."

Liz shook her head. "You don't have to…"

Andrea was already walking toward the bedroom,

and she waved over her shoulder. "See you in the morning."

They watched her enter the bedroom and close the door behind her, but neither of them spoke. Silence filled the room. Gabriel wanted to say something that would fix whatever was wrong between Liz and him, but he had no idea what that was or how to resolve it.

He flicked a hurried glance around the room as if he could find a clue to how he could begin, but he saw nothing helpful. His eyes settled on her face, and he realized that she was standing there as if holding her breath waiting for him to say something. All he could think of was how happy he was that she hadn't been hurt tonight.

He swallowed and took a step closer to her without taking his eyes off her. "Liz, I'm so thankful you weren't hurt tonight. Ever since the incident at the workshop, I've been worried sick that I failed you then, and I've been scared I'd do it again."

She frowned. "How did you fail me?"

He ran his fingers through his hair. "I should have been with you. I know it was Andrea's time to be on guard, but I should have been there. And I almost wasn't."

"What do you mean?"

She listened as he told her how he'd watched her go to the workshop but how he'd turned away from the window. "If I had stayed in place and continued watching from that window, I would have seen who locked you in that shop. I could have been there quicker."

She tilted her head to one side. "I've wondered ever

since it happened why you did come. If you thought I'd already gone back to the barn, there was no reason for you to come check on me."

He rubbed his neck and shook his head. "I've asked myself that question a hundred times since then. I don't know what it was. It was just a feeling that something wasn't right, and I needed to check it out."

A slow smile curled her lips. "You had a feeling. Was it sort of like a nagging thought that you knew wasn't going to go away until you obeyed?"

"Yeah. Exactly like that. I thought I'd take a nap, but I couldn't. I had to go see you. Does that make any sense?"

"It makes all the sense in the world. It's what I've been telling you about, Gabriel. God was urging you to come for me, to save me. I'm alive because you listened."

He felt as if his heart was about to explode in his chest. She'd never looked so beautiful as she did at that moment. The soft light of the oil lamps in the room cast a glow across her face that made every nerve in his body tingle. He took a step closer to her. "You're the most wonderful woman I've ever known in my life."

She swallowed, and he watched the muscles in her throat constrict. He wanted to reach out and touch her, but he had no idea how she would react.

"If you think that, why have you been avoiding me ever since I came home from the hospital? When you do speak to me, it's with curt words that sting."

His mouth dropped open. He hadn't realized she'd interpreted his behavior in that way. "I never meant to hurt you. I've just been so worried. I have been able to ward off four attempts on your life, and I'm terrified to think I may fail you the next time. The only thing that's been on my mind is how I can keep you safe." He was near enough now that he could touch her, and he wrapped a strand of her hair around his fingers and stroked it with his thumb.

Her eyes sparkled, and tiny breaths escaped her throat. "Then you weren't avoiding me because you were tired of me and wanted to end our friendship."

His hand released her hair, and he cupped her jaw. "Why would you think that?"

She bit down on her lip for a moment and then looked up at him. "Because I heard that you go from one woman to the other, but you grow tired of them and end it quickly."

His forehead wrinkled. "I can guess who told you that, and it's partially true. I have dated a lot of women because I'd given up on ever discovering the right one. I never found her until now."

Her eyes grew wide. "What do you mean?"

He grasped her shoulders and pulled her closer. "You're the one I've been waiting for, Liz. I'm falling in love with you, and I'm going crazy thinking that I may not keep you safe. If anything happened to you…"

The thought was so horrible he couldn't finish the sentence. She reached up and placed her palm against his cheek. "I'm falling in love with you, too, Gabriel."

He gave a low moan, wrapped his arms around her and tugged her into him. She turned her face up toward him, and he pressed his lips to hers. He'd never experienced a kiss like it in his life. The kiss deepened, and he knew this was what he'd been waiting for.

After a moment he drew back and gazed down at her. "I promise I'll protect you with my very life."

Liz stared at him. "Why didn't you tell me Gene Curtis was dead?"

He lowered his head and pressed his forehead against hers. "I didn't want you to worry about there being another hit man. I guess after tonight we know there is someone else—though I can't imagine how they found us here. So if I go off in my head and don't talk to you, know that I'm not ignoring you. I am on high alert to keep you safe."

She raised her head but stopped when her lips were almost touching his. "You don't have to do it alone, Gabriel. All I ask is that you don't keep things from me. We're starting something new, and we have to be honest with each other. You're not a solo player anymore. Now we're a team, and don't you forget it."

His throat clogged with emotion. Right now all he wanted was to bask in the reality that this incredible woman cared for him.

He'd convinced himself through the years that he would never want a life with another woman, but now he found he wanted that more than anything in the world. To have it, all he had to do was keep her alive until Daniel Shaw was convicted of murder.

The thing that concerned him was that the trial was still several weeks away, and a lot could happen in that time.

THIRTEEN

Liz sat on the rocky summit of Mount LeConte and stared out across the mountains in the distance. The trees sparkled in the early-morning light, and she smiled as she sketched the scene before her. Although heights had always scared her, she'd looked forward to coming up here. The view was spectacular, but it was made more perfect by the fact that she was sharing it with the man who sat beside her.

She glanced over at Gabriel, who was staring toward the peaks on the horizon. Even though it was a sunny day, the blue haze that gave the Smokies their name hung low over the mountaintops.

The morning rays warmed her skin, and she hugged her arms around her waist as she put aside her sketch pad for a moment and gazed at Gabriel's profile. Being here with him made everything seem brighter. Maybe it was because she was so happy. Last night Gabriel had told her about his feelings for her, and her whole world had changed.

He turned his head, and his eyes locked with hers. "What are you doing?" he asked.

"Enjoying the scenery. It's beautiful up here."

He nodded and didn't take his eyes off her. "I was just thinking the same thing."

She flushed, and she wondered if he could tell how much his words pleased her. She picked up her sketch pad and held it out to him. "Would you like to see what I've been doing?"

"Sure." He took the pad and studied it carefully before he looked up at her. "This is really good, Liz. I didn't realize you were such a good artist."

She ducked her head and smiled. "It's something I've enjoyed since I was a little girl. My father always kept a cabinet in my room filled with all kinds of art supplies when I was growing up. All my creations found their way to the refrigerator door. When it got so crowded that you could barely see the handle, my mother would place my pictures in boxes and store them in her closet. I still have all of them."

He chuckled. "My dad was a big sports fan, and he wanted me to play all kinds of sports. It's a good thing I liked it, because all my growing-up years revolved around some kind of ball game. He displayed my trophies like they were medals from the Olympics. I have all of them in a box in my garage now. I keep thinking I'll throw them away, but I can't bring myself to do that."

She reached over and grasped his arm. "Don't throw them away. Keep them to show to your son someday. He'll need to know what his daddy was like as a little boy."

He didn't say anything for a moment, and then he

scooted closer, put his arm around her waist and drew her to him to press his lips against hers. After a moment he leaned back and took a deep breath. "The day suddenly got brighter. You're lighting up my world, Liz."

She started to respond, but the sound of voices drifted on the air. They swiveled to look back at the trail that led from the lodge and saw a man and woman with a girl and boy, both of whom looked like preteens, approach. They were laughing and talking, and it reminded Liz of happy times with her parents.

They watched the family for several minutes as they explored the summit before they caught sight of her and Gabriel. The man smiled and threw up his hand. "Beautiful day for a hike."

They waved back. "It sure is," Gabriel replied.

The family stood on the edge of the cliff for several minutes as the father pointed out locations across the mountain range. Then they waved again and headed down the trail toward the lodge.

Liz watched them until they were out of sight before she spoke. "Do you think we should go check on Andrea?"

He shook his head. "No, she said she wanted to stay in bed. So let's leave her alone." He kissed Liz on the cheek. "I wished for a morning alone with you, and that's what I got. So I want to enjoy my reward, too."

Liz laughed. "What are you going to enjoy?"

His eyes sparkled. "Looking at you."

Her throat closed up for an instant, and she couldn't respond. Instead she gave him a playful shove. "Well, help yourself. I'm going to sketch."

She'd drawn just a few strokes when she heard a voice behind her. "Hello there. Enjoying the beautiful weather today?"

They glanced up to see Frank standing behind them. Liz smiled. "We are. I thought you'd be out in the woods by this time of day."

"I have been. I started out at dawn, and I've covered some of the area around here. Now I'm going to hike up to the Jump Off."

Liz shuddered. "That name makes my stomach roll. I'm scared of heights. That's why we're so far back from the edge."

Frank laughed. "Then be careful. I'd hate for you to fall off the mountain. I'll look forward to seeing you at dinner." He waved over his shoulder as he walked away.

"That guy is not eating dinner with us tonight. I'm not going to sit there and listen to him amaze you with all his adventures."

Liz laughed. "He's just trying to be nice. You might…"

She trailed off without finishing her sentence and squinted at a flash of color she'd seen in the trees near the summit.

Gabriel sat up straight and looked in the direction she was staring. "What is it?"

"I don't know. I saw something for just a moment. I just caught a flash of color, but it was the same color as that hoodie Brick was wearing last night."

He reached for the gun in his holster and started to get up. "Maybe I'd better check it out."

She grasped his arm and shook her head. "It's okay.

There's nothing there now. It could have been my imagination."

He hesitated but then sat back down. "Maybe we should go."

"No, I want to finish this sketch. Then we will."

She picked up her pad, but she knew she wasn't going to be able to concentrate. How could she when death seemed to be stalking her, and she didn't know which way it was coming from? Something told her this wasn't going to be a very productive day for sketches.

Liz glanced around at the other guests in the dining room and wondered if her happiness shone on her face. Tonight she wasn't thinking about hit men or her safety. She wanted to enjoy being with Gabriel. She was still amazed at how much had changed in twenty-four hours. Last night they had sat in stony silence across from each other, and tonight they sat side by side. In a way that's how it felt to Liz. They'd cleared the air last night, and now they were on the same page.

All during dinner he'd laughed and talked, and he'd touched her hand from time to time. But it was the way he looked at her that made her heart skip a beat. His eyes sparkled with love, and she felt as if she'd melt every time he aimed his gaze at her.

They were almost through with dessert when Andrea put her fork down and groaned. "I don't think I can stand it much longer."

Her words shocked Liz, and she stared wide-eyed at her. "What's wrong, Andrea? Is your head hurting?"

"No," she grumbled. "It's all this 'love is in the air'

routine you two are doing. I feel like a third wheel around here."

Liz laughed and shook her head. "Like I said before, you are so funny."

Andrea frowned. "Well, I don't feel very funny. I was by myself all day long while you two were out taking in the scenery. Where did you go?"

"We went up to the summit," Gabriel answered. "It's not much farther up the mountain. There's a sheer cliff up there with a view of the Smokies. Liz did a lot of sketching. I can't wait to see her paintings she does from them. If you remember, we asked you to come, but you decided to take it easy after what happened last night."

"Oh, I know," she muttered. "I'm just trying to give you a hard time." She sighed and stood up. "Anyway, I'm tired tonight. It must be the altitude. I think I'll go back to the cabin and get in bed. Do you think you can find your way without me?"

Gabriel cocked an eyebrow. "I think we can navigate that far."

She smiled. "Good. Then don't wake me when you come in."

"We'll be there soon," Liz called after her as Andrea walked from the dining room.

When she'd gone, Gabriel reached for Liz's hand and held it in his. "I had a great time today with you."

"I did, too. This is a beautiful place. I want to come back here someday when the danger is over and I have a life again."

He squeezed her hand. "We'll come back together."

Her heart thudded as her pulse rate increased. "I'd like that."

They stared at each other a second before they directed their attention back to their apple cobbler. After a moment Liz spoke. "Gabriel, do you really think Brick and his friends might be here to kill me?"

He was about to shove a bite in his mouth, but he stopped and lowered his hand. "I don't know, Liz, but the attack last night made it clear that someone's after you, and I can't overlook any suspects. Don't discount him just because he was friendly toward you before. You're too trusting and naive. It was the same with Bart Foster. I'm still not sure about him either."

She straightened her shoulders and frowned at him. "I'm not naive. I just choose to think the best of people until they prove differently."

He leaned a little closer. "Well, in my work, I've learned that you can't trust anybody until they've proven they're who they say they are."

Liz gritted her teeth. "So to your way of thinking, anybody who has a tattoo from a gang involvement in their past—even if it happened years before and they're not the same person now that they were then—is not worthy of being trusted. They have to prove they're good enough by being measured against some test you've devised to pass judgment on everybody. You even questioned Frank at dinner last night. Did he pass?"

"Yes, I checked him out on the UT website. He really does teach there, as far as I can tell."

"Oh, well, good for him. What about me? Did I pass your test?"

He tilted his head back, and he stared at the ceiling. "I can't believe this." Then he looked back at her. "Are you accusing me of being prejudiced?"

She leaned even closer. "You know the old saying about if the shoe fits…"

His eyes rounded, and then he blinked. "Wait a minute. Are we having our first fight?"

She started to tell him he was being ridiculous, but the amused expression on his face made her smile. "I guess we are."

He glanced around at the campers at the other tables, but no one seemed to be paying them any mind. "Then let's make up."

Not giving her time to protest, he pulled her to him and pressed his lips to hers. She pushed against him for all of a second or two before she poured her heart into her response. After a moment she drew back. "I'm sorry. I know you have to be careful in your job. It's just that I've always believed that all people are God's children, and we have to show them love."

"I've said it once, and I'll say it again. You are the most amazing woman I've ever known. What do you say we go sit in the rockers on the porch of our cabin and look at the moon?"

"I'd like that."

They rose from the table, and Gabriel took Liz's hand. Once outside the dining room, they paused for just a moment to stare up the moon. The clouds had cleared tonight, and Liz didn't think she'd ever seen the sky more beautiful. Maybe it was because in the midst of all the horror since Kathy's death, she had found some happiness. She hadn't thought it would ever happen to her again, but it had.

She inched closer to Gabriel and laid her head against his shoulder as they made their way back up the path to the cabin. He seemed to sense her happiness and clasped her hand tighter. He bent down and whispered, "I feel like the happiest guy in the world tonight."

"It's such a strange feeling to know that you're not alone anymore, that there's someone who cares about you and wants to make you happy. I didn't think I'd ever feel this way."

"Neither did I," he answered.

They walked in silence toward the cabin and had reached the porch when Liz stopped. "I have to go back to the dining room."

"What's wrong?"

"I left my purse on the table."

He frowned. "That's not good. If the wrong person finds it, they could steal your identity. We'd better get back there right away."

They were about to turn around when Liz felt a nudge in her back. Frowned, she glanced over her shoulder. Her heart froze at the sight of a figure behind her. He held a gun, and it was pressed to the small of her back.

"You're not going anywhere except where I tell you," he said. His soft chuckle sent chills up Liz's spine. "You really should be more observant of what you're doing, Agent Decker. You never know who's right behind you."

The breath left Liz's body, and she clutched at Gabriel's arm to keep from falling. He had been about to take a step up, and his foot still rested on the stair. "What do you want?" he growled.

"I thought that would be evident," the man replied. "I want you and this lovely witness you're protecting to meet a sudden demise. Why don't we go inside and see if we can make that happen?"

Gabriel looked down at Liz and smiled. "Don't worry, Liz. It's going to be okay."

A cruel laugh vibrated in her ear. "Yeah, keep telling yourself that. Now get inside."

Liz cast a terrified glance at Gabriel before they did as they were told.

Gabriel's mind raced with questions as he and Liz entered the cabin. How had he been so careless as to let this happen, and more important, what was he going to do about it? If he was to get them out of the situation, he couldn't panic. He needed to remain focused if they were to live.

Once inside, he and Liz walked across the room. "Stop right there," the voice commanded. The door closed, and the sound of their captor's footsteps echoed in the quiet room. He stopped several feet away from them, then spoke again. "Now pull your gun out very slowly and put it on the floor."

For an instant Gabriel wondered if he might be fast enough to get a shot off, but he thought better of it. There was too much of a risk that the man would be able to get off a shot of his own—aimed right at Liz. He had to bide his time and wait for another opportunity to present itself. He pulled the gun from his holster and laid it on the floor.

"Now, turn around."

He and Liz turned slowly, and Gabriel's eyes widened in surprise. "Frank Myers? I can't believe it."

A harsh laugh escaped the man's throat. "Believe it. I'm here to bring greetings from Daniel Shaw."

"B-but why?" Liz gasped. "You're a university professor."

Frank chuckled again. "Well, there *is* a professor named Frank Myers at the university, but he doesn't know I borrowed his name for this job. I don't think anyone will ever know except us."

Gabriel clenched his teeth and glared at the man. "You'll never get away with this. If you kill us, the FBI will come down on Daniel Shaw so hard that his drug empire will go up in smoke."

The man's harsh laugh confirmed that Gabriel's words hadn't had the effect he'd hoped. "I don't think so," he said. "It's hard to prove murder when somebody dies in what looks like an accident."

Liz inched closer to Gabriel, and he felt her body shaking. "What are you talking about?"

The man grinned. "There were a lot of witnesses that saw you two at the summit today. You were so wrapped up in each other that you barely took in your surroundings. It won't take much to conclude that you decided to take a moonlight walk up there and misjudged the edge of the cliff. All kinds of stories will be told. One witness may even say he was there sitting in the dark enjoying the view when Liz stumbled over the side, and Gabriel tried to save her. Maybe you'll even become a legend."

Gabriel heard what the man was saying, but his mind kept asking where Andrea was. The door to her bedroom was closed. That could mean that she hadn't come back here yet or that the man holding them at gunpoint had come inside the cabin earlier and killed her. His stomach dropped at the thought. Maybe she had fallen asleep and hadn't heard what was going on in the next room.

Gabriel cleared his throat. "That's a flimsy theory. Nobody's going to believe we accidentally fell off the side of the mountain." He'd spoken louder in hopes that Andrea would hear.

"We'll see." The man waved his gun toward the door. "Now let's go."

The door to the bedroom opened at that moment, and Gabriel swiveled his head to see Andrea walking into the room. She held her gun. "Watch out, Andrea!" he shouted. "He's armed."

She looked at him for a moment with a cold gaze before she directed the gun toward Liz and him. "Okay, Ray. You've taunted them enough. Quit wasting time and get on with it."

Gabriel's mouth gaped, and he couldn't move for a moment. Next to him Liz gasped. "Andrea? What are you doing?"

Liz had taken a step toward Andrea, and Gabriel reached out and held her back. "What's going on here?" he growled. "Andrea, do you know this man?"

A smirk pulled at her mouth. "I guess you can say that. We have the same boss."

The truth hit Gabriel, and he almost staggered backward. This woman he'd worked with for years and who he thought was helping him protect Liz was really employed by Daniel Shaw.

"You work for Shaw? How could you be a traitor to all the people who've trusted you?"

She shrugged. "Easy. I'm not getting rich on an agent's pay, and Daniel has promised me a big payoff for this job. I'm looking forward to living the good life on an island in the South Pacific."

"You pretended to be my friend!" Liz shouted.

Andrea nodded. "Yeah, and I do like you very much. But I like myself more. That's why I locked you in that workshop."

"B-but you were holding the horse's reins until I got back." Liz's lips quivered as she spoke.

"It didn't take much to tie the reins to a stall and get over there. I'd just barely gotten back when Gabriel came barreling in." She frowned and glowered at him. "This could have all ended that day, but you just had to play hero. Well, there's no way to save her now—or yourself."

"And did you shoot at us when we were going to Rattlesnake Creek?" Gabriel asked.

"No, that was Ray. I'm sorry to say his aim wasn't very good that day."

Gabriel's lips curled in disgust. "You're a traitor, Andrea. You swore to uphold the laws of this country, and you've traded that for a few pieces of gold. I don't think you'll ever be happy."

Andrea shook her head and laughed. "It won't matter

to you either way, because you won't be around to see it." She turned to Ray. "This has gone on long enough. Get on with it."

He smiled. "My pleasure. Okay, you two, let's go outside and take a nice leisurely walk up to the summit." He grabbed Liz's arm, pulled her in front of him and held his gun at her back. "Don't try anything, Decker, or your girlfriend will die."

The fear in Liz's eyes sucked the breath out of him. "Just take it easy," Gabriel said to Ray. "Don't do anything foolish."

Ray waved his gun toward the door. "You first. We'll follow."

Gabriel took one last look at Liz and then headed to the door. He stepped onto the porch and down the steps. Behind him he could hear Ray and Liz as they followed. When he moved onto the path in front of the cabin, he peeked over his shoulder and saw Ray and Liz right behind him, but Andrea was still standing on the porch with her gun in her hand. "Do you need me to help, or can you take care of this by yourself?" she asked.

"You can wait here for me." Ray nudged Liz forward with the gun. "Now get moving."

Gabriel turned to do as the man said. Before he could take a step, he heard movement as a figure emerged out of the shadows and tackled Ray. Gabriel spun around and saw Brick straddling Ray on the ground and his fist pounding Ray's face.

The sudden crack of a pistol split the air, and Brick's body jerked as he fell backward. Stunned, Gabriel glanced at Andrea. She still had her gun pointed in

Brick's direction. Liz had dropped down beside Brick and was bent over him.

Gabriel grabbed her arm and yanked her to her feet. "Liz, get out of here!" he yelled.

She looked up with terror-filled eyes, then ran up the path away from the cabin. Gabriel had only a second to watch her go before he stormed toward Andrea.

There was nothing he could do as he watched her aim the gun in his direction. Then his body jolted from the impact of a bullet, and he fell to the ground.

FOURTEEN

Liz's heart hammered in her chest as she ran through the darkness. She glanced around, her stomach twisting as she realized that in her haste to escape, she had run in the wrong direction—away from the office, where she might have been able to get help.

Now she was headed straight up the mountain to the summit. She scanned the darkness and tried to get her bearings, but everything looked different than it did during the day. She started to turn around and retrace her steps, and then she heard footsteps behind her. It had to be Andrea.

She glanced over her shoulder. Even in the darkness she could make out the person running toward her, and she knew it wasn't a man. Andrea was charging up the path after her. "You can't get away from me, Liz."

The words only spurred her on, and Liz bolted up the trail. She'd run perhaps fifty yards when a new fear overtook her as she realized she was approaching the summit and there was no place to hide on the rocky cliff.

She had two choices—continue on to the summit

or cut into the dense forest beside the path and try to work her way back down to the lodge while evading her pursuer.

Before she had consciously made the decision, she veered into the forest. The moonlight couldn't penetrate the thick cover of trees, and she suddenly felt as if she'd been plunged into a pit of darkness. She held up her hand, but she couldn't even see it in the pitch-black night.

Her heart lurched when she heard the snap of a twig, and she realized Andrea had followed her. The thought that she'd made the wrong choice popped into her head. Sounds carried long distances in the mountains. Every time she moved, she would broadcast her whereabouts to Andrea.

There was nothing she could do about it now. She surged forward and hoped that she could avoid hitting a tree or being stopped by a low-hanging branch—or worse, a wild animal. She shook the thoughts from her head and ran.

The problem was that in the darkness she couldn't get oriented. It took just a few minutes for her to realize she had no idea which way she should go to head back to the lodge. The only thing she could do was try to outrun Andrea, who, if the rustling sounds behind her were any indication, was gaining on her with every step.

Suddenly her foot went down in a hole, and she tumbled forward. She hit the ground with such force that for a moment she couldn't get her breath. Then she pushed to her feet. She took a few more steps but then realized running was no longer an option. At best, she'd be able to limp back to the lodge. Her ankle throbbed as if it was broken, and every step produced excruciating pain. Yet she couldn't give up.

She bit down on her lip to keep from crying out and stumbled on. After just a few yards, the forest thinned, and moonlight filtered down between the trees. A trail lay in front of her. It wasn't as well traveled as the one leading from the lodge, but either humans or animals had passed this way before. Even with the moonlight she had trouble navigating which way she should go. Did the lodge lie to her right or to her left?

There was no time to debate the issue. She had to decide and chose the right. As she staggered along the path, the footsteps behind her grew fainter. Had Andrea given up? She doubted it, and she wasn't about to turn around and check it out.

As she walked, her mind raced. Just an hour ago she and Gabriel had sat in the dining room lost in the happiness that came from falling in love. For the first time since losing her friend, Liz had been optimistic about the future. That had changed quickly with Ray whatever-his-name-was sticking a gun in her back.

Her heart thudded at the memory of Brick lying wounded on the ground and Gabriel advancing on Andrea. The fact that she had followed Liz up the trail could mean only one thing. Andrea had either killed or wounded Gabriel. And poor Brick…hurt because he'd tried to protect her.

Tears rolled down her face as she hurried on, and she prayed with each step. She didn't pray for her own safety but for Brick—and most especially for Gabriel.

At this point all she could do was place the man she loved in God's hands, but that was one of the most difficult things she'd ever done.

What if God allowed him to die? Surely He wouldn't do that, not before Gabriel had come to embrace God and follow Him in faith. Living with the thought that he'd died still questioning God's existence would be unbearable for her. So she prayed and prayed as she put one foot ahead of the other.

Her mood took a turn for the better when she spotted an opening in the trees on either side of the trail. Maybe she had made her way back to the lodge. She rushed forward as fast as she could and came to a sudden halt. Her momentary hopefulness vanished to be replaced with a shot of panic.

She had chosen the wrong path the second time, and it hadn't led her back to the lodge. It had brought her to the cliffs of Mount LeConte's summit. The rocky shelf stretched in both directions, and she pondered which way would take her back to the spot where she and Gabriel had sat earlier today. She scanned the area to try to determine where she was in relation to that place. She hadn't chosen wisely on her way up the mountain, and she wasn't sure of her choice this time.

She threw a petrified glance at the sharp drop-off and then over her shoulder. There was only one thing to do. She took a deep breath and stepped out onto the rocky shelf. She held her breath as she inched forward.

A wind whipped across the mountain, and Liz came to a stop as she braced herself against its force. After a second it calmed to a gentle breeze, and she continued moving forward. Her ankle throbbed so painfully she didn't know how she was still walking, but she couldn't stop. If she did, she'd be a sitting duck for Andrea.

After what seemed an eternity Liz caught sight of the spot where she and Gabriel had been earlier. She could make out the trail that led back to the lodge, and she breathed a sigh of relief. Now all she had to do was avoid Andrea on the way down.

A cackling laugh filled the air, and Liz froze. She'd heard that sound before, and she knew without turning around that Andrea was close behind her. She weighed her options—make a run for it and hope Andrea didn't catch her or face the woman who wanted to kill her.

The first one wasn't about to happen. She couldn't possibly run with the way her ankle felt right now. Even if she could, Andrea was in better physical shape than she was, and she'd catch up to her in no time.

Her decision made, she spun and faced Andrea. "Okay, Andrea. Let's get this over with."

Gabriel's last thought before the bullet struck him was that Liz had gotten away. He had no idea where she'd gone, but she'd run like he told her to. Would that be enough to keep her alive with Andrea on her heels? He could only hope—and pray—that God would watch over her. He lay on the cabin porch and pretended to be dead as Andrea stood over him. He held his breath and didn't move as she studied his still form. Would she check his pulse? He couldn't fake that.

But to his relief, she moved past him and hurried down the steps. He opened one eye to see what she was doing. She stood over Brick, her gun aimed at his head. *Please, Lord, don't let him be killed just for trying to help us.* Moments later, the sound of loud voices outside the dining room pierced the air, and Andrea turned her head in that direction, clearly realizing that people were approaching. Then instead of pulling the trigger, she took off in the direction that Liz had run.

"Thank You, God," he whispered, quietly but with absolute sincerity.

He wanted to go after Andrea, to stop her before she killed Liz, but he couldn't move. He fought the darkness that swirled in his head, but it was no use. He slumped into unconsciousness on the porch.

The next thing he knew, someone was bending over him. "Mister, mister. Can you hear me?"

Gabriel blinked and stared up into the face of a young man he'd seen working in the dining room earlier. He held a flashlight and peered down at him. For a moment Gabriel couldn't say anything, and then he tried to push up.

"Don't move," the young man said. "We've called for a helicopter for you and your friends."

Gabriel's heart dropped when he heard those words. Friends? Was Liz hurt?

When the young man tried to restrain him as he tried to stand again, Gabriel shoved his hand away. "Where is she?"

A puzzled look crossed the boy's face. "There isn't a woman here. There are two men, and they're both unconscious. You've been shot. You need to take it easy."

Gabriel swayed as he stood up and looked around.

Brick and Ray lay at the foot of the steps, and they both appeared to be unconscious. Several of the lodge staff knelt over them, providing some first aid. Blood trickled from the side of Brick's head, but at least it looked like he was still alive. Gabriel didn't see any blood on the hit man.

Where were Liz and Andrea? He turned his head and stared up the trail as he remembered seeing Liz running in that direction and Andrea chasing after her. He had to find them.

Gritting his teeth against the pain in his side, he looked at the young man. "I'm an FBI agent. The man who's unconscious is a hit man for a drug organization. The other one tried to help us and was shot for it. Call the park rangers and get them up here right away to put that man under arrest. In the meantime, I have another fugitive I have to capture."

He took a step to leave, but the young man caught his arm. "I don't think you're in any condition to go after anybody."

"You don't understand," Gabriel said. "I don't have a choice. The woman I love is in trouble, and I have to save her."

He pressed his hand to his side and forced his legs to move. He was well on his way up the trail to the summit when he realized he didn't have his gun. It still lay in the cabin where he dropped it when Ray was holding them at gunpoint. It was too late to worry about that now. There was no time to go back. He had to go on. He had to get to Liz in time.

As he stumbled along, he stared up at the sky and

whispered another prayer. "God, help me find her, and please take care of her until I get there."

Liz didn't move as Andrea came closer to her. When she was a few feet away, she stopped and aimed her gun at Liz's chest. "I don't want a bullet in you, but I will shoot if you try anything funny."

Liz swallowed and let her gaze drop to the gun in Andrea's hand. "Why are you doing this? Is money worth what this is going to cost you? You're a well-respected FBI agent, and you're going to exchange that title for *murderer*. Where's all the ethics and respect for the law that you're supposed to have?"

Andrea threw back her head and laughed. "I'll tell you where it is. It went down the drain one day when one of my fellow agents, a man, got the credit for closing an investigation that I had led. He got the glory and the promotion, and I got a pat on the back for all my hard work. I knew right then that I was never going to be considered a highly respected agent. I'd only be a woman agent who assisted everyone else. If I wasn't going to get rewarded by the agency, I'd have to look somewhere else. So I contacted Daniel Shaw, and I've been working for him for about three years now. I have a tidy sum hidden in an offshore account that could take care of me for life. And he's willing to double that amount if I make you go away. All I have to do is finish this one task before I disappear."

"You won't get away with this, Andrea," Liz shouted. "Gabriel will hunt you down and see that you pay."

"Gabriel?" Andrea scoffed. "Didn't you see him before we left the cabin? He was lying on the porch dead."

Tears sprang to Liz's eyes, and she wrapped her arms around her waist. "No, no. I don't believe that."

Andrea advanced toward her. "It's not going to matter in the next few minutes what you believe. Once you go over the side of this cliff, none of this will be your problem anymore—and you won't be Daniel Shaw's problem either."

Liz cast a frightened glance at Andrea and backed up a step. "Get away from me!" she screamed.

All she received in return was Andrea's high-pitched laugh.

The wind blew across the rocky cliff, and Liz stopped as it whipped about her legs. She looked down in the inky darkness below the cliff and clenched her fists at her side. She had to do something. But what?

As she inched away from the edge of the cliff, her foot dislodged a small rock, and it tumbled over the side. She could hear it striking the sides of the mountain as it dropped downward. For a fleeting moment, she wondered how far it was to the base of the mountain, and then she remembered. This mountain was over sixty-three hundred feet tall. There was no way anyone could survive the fall. And as sheer as the drop-off was at this spot, there was no chance that she'd land anywhere other than at the very bottom.

She moved a few inches away from the edge again, and Andrea stepped so close that now Liz could make out her features in the night rather than just the shadowy outline of her face. "Don't even think that you can get away. I'm wasting time here. I guess I'm going to have to push you."

Andrea reached out and grabbed Liz by the front of her blouse. "No! No! Andrea, think what you're doing!" Her voice echoed through the mountains.

"I know what I'm doing," Andrea rasped.

"Andrea!" Gabriel's voice rang out, and Liz turned her head to see him staggering to the craggy shelf of the summit. "Let her go!"

Andrea released Liz and whirled to face him. "So I didn't finish you off at the cabin after all. Well, I can take care of that right now."

She raised her gun and aimed at Gabriel, but he didn't stop. He kept coming straight at her. "I'm warning you, Gabriel. I'm going to…"

Before she could get the words out, Liz brought both her arms up underneath Andrea's and shoved her away. The gun dropped to the ground, and Andrea stumbled backward. Liz had once glimpse of her before Andrea disappeared over the side of the cliff.

Terror ripped through Liz as she realized that the momentum of the blow had caused her to lose her own balance. She reached out a hand to Gabriel as she teetered on the edge. He rushed forward, his hand outstretched, and she grabbed for him. His fingers brushed her arm, and then she was falling over the brink of the cliff.

Suddenly her body slammed against the side of the mountain, and she looked up to see what had happened. Above, Gabriel lay on his stomach, his hands wrapped around her right arm while she dangled in space.

Fear gripped her as she swung back and forth. Gabriel had hardly been able to make it across the rocks to where she was. There was no way he could pull her up in his condition. It was astounding that he was able to hold on to her at all. She closed her eyes for a moment and then gazed up at the sky. "Into Thine hands," she whispered.

Then she stared back at the man she loved hanging on to her with every bit of strength he had. In a few minutes he would be exhausted, and both of them would fall to the valley below. "Gabriel," she called out.

His head peeped over the side, and she could see the energy draining from him. His grip was becoming looser by the second.

"What?" he asked.

"I love you, and I don't want you to die. You have to let me go."

His head jerked up. "No!" he yelled. "I'll never do that."

She felt tears stream down her face. "It's time, Gabriel. I want you to let me go."

Then she closed her eyes and waited for his hand to release her.

FIFTEEN

Gabriel held on to Liz as tightly as he could, but he could feel his hands beginning to sweat. He didn't know how much longer he could keep his grip. He'd tried several times to pull her up, but every time he did, his injured side flared with pain like a hot poker had been pressed to it.

He heard her plea for him to let her go, but there was no way that was going to happen. He would follow her over the mountain before he would release her.

His body began to shake, and he knew he was nearly to the end of his endurance. He closed his eyes and grieved briefly for the future he'd imagined with Liz that now would never be. In few minutes they would be together in death.

In the last moments of his life he had to decide where he stood with his belief in God. Liz had such strength and peace. Even now when she was suspended in the air, she could speak in a calm voice and tell him to let her go. She wasn't afraid to die. He wanted the peace that she had.

His eyes still shut, he whispered, "Thank You for

giving her to me for a short time and watching over us in these last minutes of our lives."

The final word was barely out of his mouth when he heard footsteps running onto the cliff. He gasped in surprise when Clipper and Patch dropped to the ground, one on each side, and reached over the cliff. Clipper's strong hand clamped around his, and Patch's voice yelled down to Liz, "Give me your other hand!"

He watched as she raised her arm as if in slow motion, and the man grabbed it. "All right, together now," Clipper said. "Pull!"

Gabriel summoned up his last strength and tugged with all his might. With the three of them pulling together, Liz's head appeared at the edge of the cliff, and the next thing he knew, she was on the ground beside him.

He heard her gasping for breath, and then she was bent over him. "Gabriel, can you hear me?"

A smile curved his mouth as he looked from Liz to Brick's two motorcycle brothers, who'd just risked their lives to help him bring Liz to safety. He reached up and caressed her cheek. "I'm all right now."

Patch jumped to his feet. "I'll go get help. You are in no shape to walk back down."

Gabriel watched as Patch jogged down the trail and then turned his attention to Clipper, whom he'd first seen at the lodge office. That day he'd been suspicious of the men with the skull tattoos, but tonight he thought maybe Liz was right. There was some good in everyone because they were all God's children.

He held up a hand. "Thank you, Clipper."

He took Gabriel's hand. "I'm glad we got here in time."

Liz grabbed the man's hand in hers. "Thank you for saving my life. How did you happen to know we needed it?"

Clipper stroked his long beard and smiled. "We've been watching that Ray guy ever since we first saw him in the dining room. We'd seen him with some of Daniel Shaw's men before, and we knew he wasn't up here on vacation. We wanted to find out who his target was. Brick followed him last night and got there just in time to keep him from stabbing you. We were sure surprised to find out it was you, Liz."

"But there was no one there when I came to check on Andrea," Gabriel said.

"Naw, Brick took off. Figured he might have to answer too many questions. He didn't figure Ray could run away, but he did."

Gabriel tried to sit up, but Liz laid a restraining hand on his shoulder. "Is that why Brick followed us tonight and attacked Ray at our cabin?"

Clipper shook his head. "Well, he'd been watching you all day long, but he followed you tonight because we found your purse on our table in the dining room. Brick said he'd take it to you. When he didn't come back, we went looking for him. By that time the lodge employees had found him and called for a helicopter. When they told us that the wounded FBI agent had said he was pursuing a woman, we knew you needed help. So that's how we came to be at the summit."

Liz reached over and squeezed his arm. "Thank you for that. Do you know how Brick is?"

"I don't think he's hurt bad. Looked like a bullet

grazed his head, so he ought to be all right, as hard as his head is."

Liz laughed, and Clipper smiled back at her. A sudden thought flashed in Gabriel's head, and he winced. This man was a member of a motorcycle gang that the FBI had been after for years, and yet he had put his life on the line for them tonight.

Just minutes ago he and Liz had been close to death, and God had placed these men in the right place tonight to help them. It reminded him of a line from a poem that said something about God moving in mysterious ways.

"Let me add my thanks for what you did, Clipper," he said.

Clipper turned his head and stared at him. "We did it for her. I reckon my brother would be dead right now if she hadn't helped him on the trail."

Gabriel nodded. "Then let me rephrase what I just said. Thank you for saving Liz. We may find ourselves on opposite sides in the future, but for now I'd like to shake the hand of the man who saved the life of the woman I love."

He held his hand up and waited. Clipper looked at it a moment before he nodded and shook it. "For Liz," he said. Then he grinned and stared up at her. "In fact, whenever you get tired of this guy, just let me know."

Liz laughed, but Gabriel reached out and clasped her hand. "I'm afraid you've missed your chance, Clipper. I'm gonna make sure that never happens."

Liz stood at the window of the waiting room outside the hospital's surgery unit and stared out at the sun that had just peeped over the horizon. She could already tell it was going to be a glorious day in the Smokies. In fact, it was just a wonderful day to be alive.

Across the room Bill Diamond and agents from the Memphis office waited for word on Gabriel. He'd been in surgery for a while now, and she was beginning to get antsy. What if something had gone wrong? She shook her head. No, she couldn't let herself think that. She and Gabriel had been through too much for anything to happen now.

She heard footsteps running down the hall, and Dean and Gwen burst into the room. When she saw them, she rushed to them, and Gwen wrapped her arms around her. "We came as soon as we heard."

"You know what happened?"

Dean nodded. "Yeah. Bill called and told us. You've been through a rough night, but you're all right now."

Liz wanted to believe that, but when Gene Curtis was killed, Shaw's organization had just sent somebody else to finish the job. She wondered who would come next. Before she could voice her concerns, Bill walked over and grasped Dean's hand.

"Good to see you, Dean. Thanks for helping watch over Liz while she's been here."

Dean smiled. "It's been our pleasure. I still can't believe that Andrea worked for Shaw, though."

Bill sighed and nodded. "Neither can I. I always thought she did a good job. I guess we'll be checking all the cases she worked on to see if they have links to Shaw. I'm just thankful that Gabriel and Liz are okay. This case is going to have a big effect on his career. It should solidify his chance of getting that director's job in Texas."

Liz's stomach roiled at the words. She'd forgotten about the promotion. What did that mean for Gabriel and her? They'd professed their love for one another, but at the time she'd imagined them living in Memphis. Could a long-distance relationship survive when he was settling in to such an important job?

She swallowed and pulled to her full height. It didn't matter what happened when they got back to Memphis. The important thing was that they were both alive, and they were in love.

The sound of a throat being cleared pierced the room, and she turned to see Clipper, Brick and Patch standing at the door. They stared at Bill Diamond, who didn't break eye contact with them. The air crackled with tension.

Before anybody could speak, she hurried forward, grabbed Clipper's hand and pulled him into the room. Brick and Patch followed. "I want you to meet my friends," she said. "This is Dean, who owns Little Pigeon Ranch, and this is his wife, Gwen. I've been staying with them while I've been here."

Each of the bikers shook Dean's hand, and then they turned their attention to Gwen. "Ma'am," Clipper said as he shook her hand. Brick and Patch echoed his greeting.

Liz took a deep breath and put her hand on Bill Diamond's arm. "And this is…"

"I know who he is," Clipper said, but he didn't reach for Bill's hand.

Bill let his gaze rake over the three men before he spoke. "I want to thank you for saving Miss Madison and my agent."

Clipper gave a curt nod. "No problem." He turned back to Liz. "We're on our way back to Memphis and wanted to check on you before we left." He grinned at her. "We came up to get away and hike the mountains for a few days, but you've made it a trip we won't ever forget."

Tears welled in Liz's eyes as she looked at each of them. "I don't know how I can ever thank you for all you've done for me. Most people in your position would probably have ignored the whole situation, and yet you chose to risk your lives. I'll never forget you."

Clipper smiled at her. "You helped our brother. We weren't about to let anything happen to you."

He stuck out his hand, but Liz grinned and shook her head. "We can do better than that."

She put her arms around Clipper and hugged him. "I know God sent you and your brothers to save me. We're all His children, and He loves you, too. I'm going to be praying for you."

He swallowed as he released her, but he didn't say anything. She then did the same for Brick. "You take care of yourself, and make sure you have candy in your pockets in case somebody steals yours again. I'll be praying for you."

He ducked his head and stared at the floor. "I will, Liz."

Then she hugged Patch. "Your hand stretched out to me was the sweetest sight I've ever seen. I will never forget how safe I felt when you took hold of me. Thank you, and I'll be praying for you, too."

The three men stared at her for a moment before Clipper glanced at Bill. "By the way, Diamond, you ain't got to worry about that contract on Liz anymore. She's safe."

"How did that happen, Clipper?" Bill asked.

He shrugged. "We knew a guy who was glad to do us a favor."

Before Liz could ask what that meant, the men strode toward the door. Clipper held up his hand and stopped them before they could exit and then walked back to Liz. He stared down at her a moment before he spoke.

"Liz, all my life I've tried to live true to who I really am and not care what other people thought, but with you it's different. I want you to know that the Skulls is not a motorcycle gang. We're a club. We're a closed fraternity of brothers who look after each other and after each other's families. Folks look at how we dress, at our hair and tattoos, and they judge us." He eyed Bill Diamond. "And the FBI can keep trying to come up with something on us, but they ain't going to find anything. Because there's nothing there. I just wanted you to know."

Then he turned, and the three men left the room. Liz stared after them, then looked back at Bill Diamond. "Did you hear that?"

"I heard."

"And do you believe him?"

Bill sighed. "We've looked for several years, but we can't find anything. I don't know what to believe, Liz."

She turned back toward the hall, but the men were

already out of sight. "Well, *I* believe him. They could have easily gone over that cliff with Gabriel and me, but they hung on and pulled us to safety. There has to be a lot of good in someone who's willing to risk his life to save someone else."

She paused as another thought struck her. "Do you think he was telling the truth about the contract being lifted?"

Bill smiled. "Yeah, I do believe that. There's a lot that goes on behind the scenes in their world."

"Then I owe them even more," she said. "Do you think I'll ever see them again?"

"You may not see them, but I have a feeling that they'll be watching out for you. You've just come under their protection, and they take that commitment seriously. But we don't need to think about that today. Right now we have to celebrate that this case turned out all right."

Liz nodded, but she couldn't rid herself of the thought that Gabriel was about to go to Texas and she would be staying in Memphis. Perhaps this case could have had a happier ending.

She didn't have time to ponder that, because at that moment the doctor walked in. He stopped in surprise when he saw everyone gathered in the waiting room. "Are all of you here with Mr. Decker?"

Bill Diamond stepped forward. "We are. How is he?"

"He's doing fine. The bullet had a clean exit and didn't hit any vital organs. From what I hear, though, he was quite the hero on that mountain. I can't imagine how he managed to get up and walk with that injury, let alone help pull a woman to safety."

Bill smiled. "He's an exceptional agent. When can I see him?"

"He's in the recovery room, and we'll have him in a regular room in an hour or so. Right now, though, he wants to see his girlfriend. He threatened to get up and walk out here if I didn't let her come back there."

"Girlfriend?" Gwen gasped.

Everyone turned, and they stared at Liz as if she had two heads. She lifted her chin. "Yes, girlfriend. Gabriel and I decided we like each other." She paused a second. "*Really* like each other."

Gwen was the first to react. She laughed and clapped her hands together before she engulfed Liz in a big hug. Then she held Liz at arm's length and stared into her eyes. "Good for you. Now get back there and see that handsome man. We'll be waiting right here."

Liz nodded, then hurried from the room and followed the doctor through the doors that led to the recovery room. He smiled at her and motioned for her to go inside. "Don't stay too long. You can be with him later once we've settled him in his room."

She took a deep breath and walked into the room. Her heart pricked when she saw him lying on the bed. He didn't look like the brave, strong man she'd been falling in love with for the past few weeks. Monitors attached to his body beeped as she stopped by his bed, and she studied the screen where his blood pressure, heart rate and other vital signs were being displayed.

Suddenly the memory of the events of the night before returned, and tears clouded her vision. Her body shook as she recalled how it had felt when she was dangling over that cliff and Gabriel was holding on to her. He'd been weak, but he'd held on. How could she ever thank him enough for that?

He looked so pale lying there, his eyes closed and his chest rising and falling. His hair was plastered to his forehead, and she brushed it back in place. The movement caused him to stir, and he opened his eyes. A smile curled his mouth.

"They let you come in." The words were barely above a whisper. "I'm glad you're here."

She stroked his head again. "I am, too. Thank you for holding me and not letting me go."

His smile grew larger, and he closed his eyes. "I'll always hold on to you."

His breathing became even, and she knew he'd fallen back asleep. She pulled a chair up beside his bed, sat down and took his hand in both of hers. She brought his hand to her lips and kissed his fingers one after another.

Then she rested her head on the bed beside him and held on to the man she loved as she drifted off to sleep.

Two weeks later Gabriel stood in the entry of Dean and Gwen's house and waited for Liz to come downstairs. What could be taking her so long? She'd told him thirty minutes ago that she was almost ready to go.

Dean walked out of the kitchen and came to where he stood. "Liz still getting ready to leave?"

Gabriel sighed. "Yeah. How could it take one person that long to get ready? She's been at it for hours."

Dean laughed and shook his head. "You'd better get used to it. I think one of the secret pleasures that women have is keeping their men waiting."

Gabriel nodded. "I guess I should be happy she's here at all. If things had turned out differently on that mountain…"

"But they didn't," Dean interrupted, "and you've got to quit tormenting yourself with what-ifs. Just be thankful for how it did work out." He paused for a minute. "Which makes me think of something I've been meaning to ask you. What's the latest news about the case?"

"I heard from Ben this morning. Ray, whose last name turned out to be Scott, has been arraigned for attempted murder and will have a court date set in the next few days. After his trial here, he'll go back to Memphis to face some outstanding charges there. It looks like he may be in jail for years to come."

"And Andrea? What about her?"

Gabriel exhaled a big breath. "They recovered her body and sent it home to her parents. I understand they are devastated. They were so proud of their FBI agent daughter. Bill says they're still going through her files to see if she'd given special consideration to any of her cases related to Daniel Shaw."

"I still can't believe she was working for him," Dean said.

"I know. I can't, either, and I worked beside her in a lot of cases."

Dean put his hands in his pockets and stared at Gabriel. "Has Bill said anything to you about the promotion? I know they've been considering you."

He nodded. "Yeah. He called me this morning and offered me the director's job in Texas."

"And you took it?"

"I did. It's a great opportunity for me."

"Have you told Liz yet?"

"I'm getting ready to," he said as he glanced at his watch and then back up the stairs toward Liz's room. "I think I'm going to have to tell her to hurry. At this rate it's going to be night when we get back to Memphis."

"You will keep a close watch over her until she testifies in the trial next week, won't you? Liz has become very special to Gwen and me."

Gabriel laughed and slapped Dean on the back. "You don't have to worry about that. I intend to watch over her for the rest of my life."

Then he hurried up the stairs and down the hall to Liz's room. He stopped at the door and gazed at her as she fastened a suitcase that sat on the bed. For a minute all he could do was stare at her. She looked like a true princess standing there with the sun shining in the window and reflecting off her hair.

The road to their happily-ever-after had been filled with danger, but just like in a true fairy tale, goodness and love had triumphed in the end. And best of all, the princess had chosen him. She had brought so many things into his life, not the least of which was his newfound faith. He'd never been so happy or so at peace in his life.

He stepped into her room. "Ready to go?"

She turned and smiled at him. He could see the shimmer of moisture in her eyes, and he took her in his arms and pulled her close. "Having trouble saying goodbye?"

She bit her lip and nodded. "I've really come to love this place."

He tucked her against his chest and kissed the top of her head. "It's not a final goodbye. We're going to come back here. After all, it seems like home now."

She looked up at him and smiled. "I feel like I've learned so much since I've been here. Now it's time to go back and make Daniel Shaw pay for what he did."

"Are you scared about testifying?"

She shook her head. "No. It's something I have to do." Then she grinned up at him. "I was thinking this morning that I've become so used to people calling me Liz Madison I may not recognize my real name when the court calls Elizabeth Kennedy to the stand."

Gabriel laughed. "So, what's it going to be when all of this is over? Madison or Kennedy?"

She smiled. "I haven't decided yet."

He put his hand under her chin, lifted her face up and stared down into her eyes. "I have a suggestion. How about changing it to Liz Decker? I think that has a nice ring to it."

Her eyes grew wide, and her mouth dropped open. "Gabriel, are you…"

"Proposing?" he finished for her. "Yeah, I am. I got the job in Texas, Liz. I want you to go with me as my wife. What do you think?"

She put her arms around his neck and tugged his head down so that their lips were almost touching. "I think that's the best deal I've had in a long time. How about we seal the bargain with a kiss?"

He smiled. "Anything you want, Princess."

"Back at you, Prince Charming," she said before his lips captured hers.

As the kiss deepened, he remembered telling himself once that he was no Prince Charming, but as long as Liz thought he was, that was all that mattered to him.

* * * * *

Be sure to pick up the other stories in

SMOKY MOUNTAIN SECRETS:
IN A KILLER'S SIGHTS
STALKING SEASON

Find more great reads at www.LoveInspired.com

Dear Reader,

I hope you enjoyed reading *Ranch Hideout*. I wrote this story because I wanted to impress upon readers the importance of relying on God. In this story Liz faced what seemed to be an insurmountable problem, but she knew she wasn't facing it alone. She did what we all should do when we find ourselves facing something that threatens to overwhelm us—she put her faith in God. He has told us that He is sufficient to meet our needs, make our lives richer and give us peace. If you haven't done so, I pray you will put your trust in God and experience the strength and peace that will come from it.

Sandra Robbins

COMING NEXT MONTH FROM
Love Inspired® Suspense

Available May 9, 2017

SHERIFF
Classified K-9 Unit • by Laura Scott

Back in her hometown investigating the disappearance of a colleague, FBI K-9 agent Julianne Martinez doesn't expect to witness a jailbreak and become a target—or to work with her former love, Sheriff Brody Kenner, to bring in the fugitive.

AMISH REFUGE
Amish Protectors • by Debby Giusti

On the run after escaping her kidnappers, Miriam Miller takes refuge in an Amish community. Will hiding in the home of Abram Zook and his sister save her life—even as she loses her heart and begins to embrace the Amish faith?

CALCULATED VENDETTA
by Jodie Bailey

When Staff Sergeant Travis Heath rescues his ex-girlfriend, Staff Sergeant Casey Jordan, from a mugger, a killer begins hunting them. And with attempts on their lives escalating, they must figure out who has a vendetta against them...and why.

TEXAS TAKEDOWN
by Heather Woodhaven

Marine biologist Isabelle Barrows's research findings could put her institute on the map, but someone will resort to anything—even murder—to steal it before she can present it at a conference. And her only hope of surviving is relying on her former friend, Matt McGuire, for help.

CRASH LANDING
by Becky Avella

After stumbling on a drug-smuggling operation, rancher Sean Loomis and pilot Deanna Jackson must flee. But with men trying to kill them and a dangerous wildfire raging around them, can they make it out with their lives?

SHATTERED SECRETS
by Jane M. Choate

Narrowly escaping thugs who held her at knifepoint, lawyer Olivia Hammond turns to the man who once broke her heart, bodyguard Sal Santonni, for protection. But can they find her kidnapped boss and track down the person who's after Olivia before the attacks turn fatal?

The low rumble of a car engine caused FBI agent Julianne
Martinez to freeze in her tracks. She quickly gave her
K-9 partner, Thunder, the hand signal for "stay." The Big
Thicket region of east Texas was densely covered with
trees and brush. This particular area of the woods had
also been oddly silent.

Until now.

Moving silently, she angled toward the road, sucking
in a harsh breath when she caught a glimpse of a black-
and-white prison van.

The van abruptly stopped with enough force that it
rocked back and forth. Frowning, she edged closer to get
a better look.

There was a black SUV sitting diagonally across the
road, barricading the way.

Julianne rushed forward. As she pulled out her weapon,
she heard a bang and a crash followed by a man tumbling
out of the back of the prison van. The large bald guy
dressed in prison orange made a beeline toward the SUV.

Another man stood in the center of the road pointing a weapon at the van driver.

A prison break!

"Stop!" Julianne pulled her weapon and shot at the gunman. Her aim was true, and the gunman flinched, staggering backward, but didn't go down.

He had to be wearing body armor.

The gunman shot the driver through the windshield, then came running directly at Julianne.

She ducked behind a tree, then took a steadying breath. Julianne eased from one tree to the next as Thunder watched, waiting for her signal.

Crack!

She ducked, feeling the whiz of the bullet as it missed her by a fraction of an inch.

After a long moment, she was about to risk another glance when the gunman popped out from behind a tree.

"Stop right there," he shouted. "Put your hands in the air."

Angry that she hadn't anticipated the gunman's move, Julianne held his gaze.

"Put your hands in the air!" he repeated harshly.

"Fire that gun and I'll plant a bullet between your eyes," a familiar deep husky Texan drawl came from out of nowhere.

Brody Kenner?

Don't miss
SHERIFF by Laura Scott,
available wherever
Love Inspired® Suspense ebooks are sold.

www.LoveInspired.com

Turn your love of reading into rewards you'll love with
Harlequin My Rewards